Doors In

Doors In

The Fairy Tale World of George MacDonald

ROLLAND HEIN

Foreword by Olga Lukmanova

CASCADE *Books* · Eugene, Oregon

DOORS IN
The Fairy Tale World of George MacDonald

Cascade Books
An Imprint of Wipf and Stock Publishers
199 W. 8th Ave., Suite 3
Eugene, OR 97401

www.wipfandstock.com

PAPERBACK ISBN: 978-1-5326-4381-1
HARDCOVER ISBN: 978-1-5326-4382-8
EBOOK ISBN: 978-1-5326-4383-5

Cataloguing-in-Publication data:

Names: Hein, Rolland, author.

Title: Doors in : the fairy tale world of George MacDonald / Rolland Hein.

Description: Eugene, OR: Cascade Books, 2018 | Includes bibliographical references.

Identifiers: ISBN 978-1-5326-4381-1 (paperback) | ISBN 978-1-5326-4382-8 (hardcover) | ISBN 978-1-5326-4383-5 (ebook)

Subjects: LCSH: MacDonald, George, 1824–1905—Religion. | Fiction—Religious aspects—Christianity. | Spiritual life in literature.

Classification: PR4969 .H45 2018 (paperback) | CALL NUMBER (ebook)

Manufactured in the U.S.A.   12/14/18

Men do not heed the rungs by which men climb
Those glittering steps, those milestones upon time,
Those tombstones of dead selves, those hours of birth,
Those moments of the soul in years of earth.

—"Biography," John Masefield

Contents

Foreword

I hope in every person's life there is a moment when she finds a great teacher. For me, one such moment was back in 1995, in my university's research library. I had come looking for something completely unrelated and was browsing around the shelves, when my half-distracted glance lighted on a neat row of paperbacks with the name I recognized. I was a relatively new Christian in post-Soviet Russia but I had already read enough of C. S. Lewis to remember the Scotsman from *The Great Divorce* who apparently had done for Lewis what Lewis himself was now doing for me. My first MacDonald book came home with me that day, and . . . how does one describe love, and relief, and that bracing and sweet sense of goodness and cleanliness, when cobwebs are swept from your brain and your heart and you emerge better and stronger after the encounter? I now understood why the befuddled and battered Jane Studdock from *That Hideous Strength*, when she finally got to a place of rest, asked for MacDonald's Curdie books: few other things can bathe a tired soul in their wholesome goodness and help one regain some clarity of mind by the bright lucidity of their moral imagination. Lewis's master was now my master too.

Now, more than twenty years later, I know him immeasurably better, and the effect never fades. His sermons are among the best I have ever read, his novels remain a treasure trove (and I hope to translate at least seven more to add to the three already completed—maybe when I retire!), and I constantly recommend and give away his fairy tales to childlike friends. Just yesterday, talking to someone about a more grounded understanding of God's love, I found myself saying, "Of course, for me it all started with George MacDonald . . . ." No one writes about the deep fatherhood and essential childlikeness of God quite as compellingly, so it is always a delight to see people discover him for the first time and exclaim in starry-eyed wonder, "Where have I been all this time? Why didn't anyone tell me about this? What should I start with? What shall I read next?"

When such excited questions are asked in the many online groups of MacDonald's aficionados, longtime readers recommend their personal favorites which vary; but what never varies is that answers always include the fairy tales and fantasies: *The Princess and the Goblin,* with its sequel *The Princess and Curdie, The Wise Woman* (a.k.a. *The Lost Princess* or *The Double Story*), *The Golden Key, The Light Princess, At the Back of the North Wind*—and of course, *Phantastes* and *Lilith,* the two great "bookends" of MacDonald's fantasy writing.

What also almost never varies is that many of these exclamations and requests are later followed by baffled confessions which can be condensed into One Big Question: "What does this mean?" Sometimes people are uncertain about the imagery, sometimes about the meaning of certain symbols, and sometimes about the author's theology. Who is the North Wind? What does the golden key symbolize, exactly? And does MacDonald really imply that repentance and redemption are possible after death? Or that what we see as evil is, in fact, "the best shape, which, for the person and his condition at the time, could be assumed by the best good"? Sometimes well-meaning and godly Christians are even a bit frightened: they can't help feeling the power of the stories and their inherent truthfulness . . . but isn't it all a little too wild, a little too undefined, a little too . . . good?

Over the last thirty or forty years, ever since the name of George MacDonald resurfaced in Christian and literary circles and began to gain new popularity and respect, various interpretations of his fantasy writing have abounded, including contributions from folklore and fantasy experts, feminist literary critics, Vladimir Propp-loving structuralists (of which I am one), theologians, psychoanalysts, postmodern thinkers looking for the subversive and controversial, and many others of every stamp. This new volume from Dr. Rolland Hein, a leading MacDonald scholar and his faithful biographer, offers yet another reading of those key fairy tales and fantasies that people are likely to have heard of and often start with, precisely because it is just too easy to get lost in the interpretations, and one needs a reliable guide, especially in the beginning.

Much as Virgil walked alongside Dante, and MacDonald showed Lewis around Heaven, Dr. Hein walks the reader through these lovely but sometimes puzzling narratives, anticipating difficulties, answering questions, and pointing out subtle gems that otherwise might go unnoticed.

His unmatched knowledge of MacDonald's life and thought and his painstaking labor on the writer's biography and the variorum edition of *Lilith*, make him an ideal guide—first of all, because due to his lifelong and ever-deepening engagement with the texts, he can see the whole body of MacDonald's work as one beautiful interconnected world and is thus able to give insights that would escape a less informed reader. Under his guidance, we begin to see connections between the air-fish in *The Golden Key*, the animals in the Curdie books, and the strange monsters of *Lilith*, as MacDonald's main themes and persistent imagery—the moon, the library, mirrors, water and swimming, children, night and sleep, etc.—grow more and more multi-faceted, acquiring new levels of meaning.

I often joke that teachers are harvesters and bakers combined: they glean what they can from the rich fields of world's literature, history, and culture, grind and process it all in their minds, and in the end produce loaves that they then hand out to others to save them the time and effort of their own harvesting and baking. Not everyone has the learning and the patience to really dig into Novalis and Browning or to trace Dante's tiny reference to Thomas Aquinas, so we, on the receiving end, are grateful that someone else has done the digging and now illumines our way in. Dr. Hein helps us make inroads into philosophy and literature by reminding us of Plato's myth of the cave and demonstrating its potential significance in many of the stories, by quoting Blake, Burns, and Wordsworth (on all of whom MacDonald frequently lectured), and by drawing parallels with other poets and thinkers of the age, both to acquaint us with the literary, intellectual, and ecclesiastical climate of the time and to underline the universal nature of MacDonald's poetic insight. Those who know and appreciate Dostoyevsky, Dickens, Thoreau, Chesterton, and Emily Dickinson, will relish the exercise, and those who do not will learn a whole lot and maybe will be intrigued enough to try and open these further "doors in."

Sometimes we moderns also need assistance because we simply do not have the education that people in MacDonald's time had. It doesn't mean we know less, but it does mean that most of us have probably never read Horace or Homer in the original, and thus hidden meanings of names like "Anodos" or "Bulika" are not immediately transparent. Those of us engaged in translating MacDonald into other languages and cultures especially appreciate the help—precisely because otherwise we may not be able to catch classical allusions or spot a quote. Also, symbols that were fresh and obvious in MacDonald's day may have retreated into the past, becoming obscure or getting superseded by modern associations. Bible stories that most people in MacDonald's time probably knew from early childhood are not necessarily familiar, and even understanding something as simple as a rainbow can't be taken for granted anymore. So, to make sure no one is lost along the way, Dr. Hein refers the reader to relevant biblical passages, showing familiar (or not so familiar) teaching restated and reshaped into captivating pictures. As a result, these Bible-infused symbols become for us almost a school of reading the Scripture imaginatively, of allowing its power to engage with our whole selves. What is "the beauty of holiness," for instance, but a fragrant fire of roses that burns, and cleanses, and gives new life and the gift of discernment?

"But wait!" someone will protest. "Can't I just read the stories and enjoy them without going into the difference between the symbolic and the allegorical, without looking up the word "Buildungsroman" and without a trip down the literary and theological lane? Certainly. Just like Christ's own parables or, indeed, the gospel and even Christ himself, a good fairy tale can be encountered on different levels. You can simply enjoy it, accept it without questions or reflection, let it wash over you like music, and, not unlike Mr. Vane, forever wander in the magical wood, reveling in its sweet melancholy and mistaking the feeling of the numinous for the Numinous itself. Or, despite the initial attraction, somewhere along the line you may find yourself too puzzled or too lost and thus abandon the story in vague distaste. Or you can truly love it, and, as with a favorite piece of music, want to see and hear more, tracing each intricate pattern so that, ultimately, you are able to, as modern Ignatians put it, "see clearer, love dearer, and follow nearer." To those curious, Dr. Hein gladly uncovers some of MacDonald's techniques for pulling the reader into the story, explaining how things work together and teaching us, inattentive readers of the gadget age, often untrained to notice details and connections, to draw general conclusions that would then make springboards for further thought.

However, like all great teachers—and like MacDonald's own Mr. Raven, Wise Women, and Great-great-grandmother Irene—Dr. Hein only shows you where to look, but doesn't tell you what to see. In this, he follows the philosophy of MacDonald himself, reiterating again and again that no reading is final, and placing emphasis on helping the reader "see the theological import of each fantasy." He is never dogmatic in his statements and is careful to describe what specific images might "suggest" in the light of what he knows about MacDonald's artistic vision, without laying down the law as to how things should be interpreted. He echoes "the Victorian mythmaker's" own sentiment that a good fairy tale is akin to a good sonata: we feel its meaning intensely and receive it not so much through the intellect as by the heart, yet can't help reflecting on it. As with the knowable-unknowable God, we want to probe further and further into the real depths and to find the immeasurable treasures, hidden in the revelation and open only to those who have eyes to see and ears to hear: those who will take the trouble to ask the necessary questions.

In one of his letters, C. S. Lewis advises his friend about a great book: "Do get it and don't mind if you don't understand everything the first time. It deserves reading over and over again."[1] That's exactly what I would say about George MacDonald's fairy tales and fantasies, for, in Dr. Hein's words, they offer "many mythic moments to the attentive reader." And whether you're a longtime lover of George MacDonald's work or a beginner in the paths of his Fairy Land, this new volume by Dr. Hein will be of much help as a guide and companion in your journey through MacDonald's rich magical world. Bon voyage! And may you emerge from this truly transformative encounter desiring to know more and love better.

Olga Lukmanova
Associate Professor,
English Department,
N.A. Dobrolubov State Linguistic University
of Nizhny Novgorod, Russia

1. Hooper, ed., *They Stand Together,* 479.

Preface

I well remember my early encounters with George MacDonald's fantasies. I was the pastor of a small fundamentalist congregation in a semi-rural setting, having recently earned a seminary degree, and—as I had time—I was taking graduate courses in literature at a nearby university. I was concentrating on the nineteenth century, loving the plethora of novels, poetry, and essays one had to master for a degree. I read some of MacDonald's works, liked them, and then I came onto *Phantastes*.

It fascinated me, but it was a puzzle. It was different from anything I had read, and I couldn't fit it into any of the genres I was familiar with. Yet somehow it drew me into it, so that I found myself returning to it and being captivated by the way in which it spoke to me on a level quite beyond that of the other works I was reading, provocative as I conceived the others to be. Here was something that seemed to bypass my intellect and arouse emotions that, I'm afraid, I had been stifling.

I owe an immense debt to my upbringing in the strict fundamentalist church in which my parents were quite active, and to the training I received from the denominational seminary I attended, and I certainly do not want to discredit that. But it did little for my imagination. One day I happened to pick up a little volume by J. B. Phillips entitled *Your God Is Too Small*, and it helped me to realize my Christianity was too much a narrow intellectual affair that did not do life justice. It began to dawn upon me that my commitment was too much to an intellectual grasp of an abstract system of doctrines that really existed quite apart from life itself and was inadequately speaking to the true realities of experience. My understanding of Christian truth was too narrow because it was not allowing my imagination to engage reality, and, as I have come to realize since, it is through the imagination that one catches glimpses of Ultimate Reality. I was starving my spirit.

That which kept me coming back to *Phantastes* was simply my hungering imagination crying out to be allowed the role it so strongly desired to play in shaping my personal relationship to God. I seized upon this fantasy with great delight and allowed it to beckon me to aspects of the spiritual life for which my soul longed. I began to see that MacDonald masterfully uses the elaborate metaphor of Fairy Land as a map for the reader to explore the soul-delighting adventures that await a person who allows the Holy Spirit to illumine the spiritual nature of every aspect of our physical world.

The more I read MacDonald's fantasies the more vibrant my spiritual life became, for they offered me those "moments of the soul" for which I secretly longed: the Princess Irene's encounter with her great-great-grandmother when she climbed high enough, Curdie thrusting his hands into the rose-fire while the ancient lady wept, Tangle's finally arriving at the Old Man of the Fire to find him to be a baby arranging building blocks—the list could go on and on. Such were moments that caught the breath, emitting an aura quite beyond the reach of my intellect fully to explain, but which impacted me with soul-exciting truths. Hence my motivation in writing this little volume: simply to share something of what I have seen, with a view to helping my readers catch imaginative glimpses of those truths that will speak most powerfully to them, wherever they might be on our mutual journey to spiritual maturity.

Acknowledgments

I would be seriously remiss if I did not acknowledge the debt I owe to those many friends that have joined me in reading and discussing these fantasies when we have met together in Saturday morning sessions at the Marion E. Wade Center on the Wheaton College campus. Collected there are the works and manuscripts of C. S. Lewis, together with those of six other authors who impacted him, MacDonald being one of them. Our interactions have been for me highly enjoyable and profitable; without them this little volume may well not have come into being. I also thank Olga Lukmanova for taking time from her busy teaching schedule to write a foreword, Justice Carmen for volunteering to design the cover, John Larson for helpful comments on parts of the manuscript, Bill MacKey and Heather Hein for helping with the formatting, and Ted Lewis for his encouragement and advice.

Introduction

George MacDonald begins an article on Browning's poem "Christmas Eve" by quoting from one of Goethe's poems, in which he states that there are two approaches to the task of reading a poem. The one is like trying to look into a church from the outside through one of its stained glass panels: the interior appears dim, dark, and forbidding. The second is like going inside, beholding the "rainbow bright" colors of the windows, seeing the stories they portray, and experiencing the "gracious splendor" of the truths they reveal. Such, he suggests, is the nature of a person's experience with art.

The metaphor aptly applies to all truly Christian fantasies, such as *At the Back of the North Wind*. To approach them simply intellectually is to see them from the outside, as it were; they appear dim, and perhaps silly: attempts to prettify truths by cloaking them with a tale. The trick is to abstract whatever truth the author is attempting to tell, clarify it in prose statement, and discard the story itself. Taking such an approach is to lock oneself out from deeply satisfying encounters with ultimate Reality that an imaginative entering into the fantasy affords.

To see the story itself as expendable is to overlook the basic fact that beauty imaginatively received is the most appropriate home for truth. To attempt to separate truth from beauty is to impoverish truth. Emily Dickinson captures this verity in her poem:

> Tell all the truth, but tell it slant,
> Success in circuit lies;
> Too bright for our infirm delight,
> The truth's superb surprise.
> As Lightning to the children eased
> With explanation kind,
> The truth must dazzle gradually

Or every man be blind.[1]

It is the imagination that supplies the "circuit" of the story, and the reader must get inside a story, experience it imaginatively, in order to really perceive the truths involved. The process is one of indirection. Experience precedes understanding. The creeds of Christendom appear forbidding and meaningless until that personal encounter makes them live. Just as Christ is a person to be personally met and received in the heart, not an abstraction merely to be affirmed, Christian fantasies must be experienced to be understood.

George MacDonald discovered this truth as a young man, and he made it his lifelong purpose to help people discover it for themselves. Such is the motivating force shaping each of the fantasies he wrote. He repeatedly uses the fairy tale genre to fulfill this purpose; it allows him to express his vision of truth fully with compelling imaginative power, while enabling him to avoid using conventional Christian jargon.

Having been raised in northern Scotland under the intellectually doctrinaire rigors of Scottish Presbyterianism, as a student in the early 1840s at King's College, Aberdeen, he was restless and searching for a more satisfying orientation to life. His discovery of the German romantic writers, such as Novalis and Hoffmann, revolutionized his thinking, for they illustrated for him the indispensable role which the imagination must play in developing a truly viable Christian faith.

Most of MacDonald's fantasies are fine examples of the fairy tale genre. As a child he loved the rich tradition of Scotch and Irish—Celtic and Gaelic—fairy tales, and his genius lies in his ability to create the unique atmosphere and tone that produces the singular effects of that literary type. Fairy tales convey their meanings in a unique manner. They speak to the reader's inner life, posing images and events that appeal to the subconscious and therefore address a person's unique inner struggles and concerns.

They have a very important function in the life of children, helping them to come into a healthy relationship to the mysteries of life, achieving effects quite beyond the ability of realistic stories. Bruno Bettelheim explains:

> Fairy tales, unlike any other form of literature, direct the child to discover his identity and calling, and they also suggest that experiences are needed to develop his character further. Fairy tales

---

1. Johnson, ed., *The Complete Poems of Emily Dickinson*, #1129.

intimate that a rewarding, good life is within one's reach despite adversity—but only if one does not shy away from the hazardous struggles without which one can never achieve true identity.[2]

What is true for the child is no less true for an adult when the tales are focused upon adult concerns and needs. They help a person feel the true nature of one's soul before God, the nature of a right relationship with him, and the satisfying excitement of a proper response to his expectations. MacDonald understood this. He was keenly aware that certain childlike dimensions are necessary components to a healthy spiritual life. He often refers to Christ's statements in this regard.[3] He remarked: "For my part, I do not write for children, but for the childlike, whether of five, of fifty, or seventy-five."[4]

Bettelheim explains further:

> In a fairy tale, internal processes are externalized and become comprehensible as represented by the figures of the story and its events. . . . Fairy stories do not pretend to describe the world as it is, nor do they advise what one ought to do. . . . The fairy tale is therapeutic because the patient finds his *own* solutions, through contemplating what the story seems to imply about him and his inner conflicts at this moment in his life. The content of the chosen tale usually has nothing to do with the patient's external life, but much to do with his inner problems, which seem incomprehensible and hence unsolvable.[5]

This is precisely the way MacDonald's tales function.

For the adult reader of these tales, the intellect and the imagination work in tandem. In "The Fantastic Imagination," MacDonald expresses it well: "What we mean to insist upon is, that in finding out the works of God, the Intellect must labor, workman-like, under the direction of the architect, Imagination." When a reader's intellect is working subservient to the imagination, the full person is involved. MacDonald's thought continues:

> In very truth, a wise imagination, which is the presence of the spirit of God, is the best guide that man or woman can have; for it is not the things we see the most clearly that influence us the most powerfully; undefined, yet vivid visions of something beyond,

2. Bettelheim, *The Uses of Enchantment*, 24.

3. E.g., Matt 18:2–6.

4. "The Fantastic Imagination," in Hein, ed., *The Heart of George MacDonald*, 426.

5. Ibid., 25.

something which eye has not seen nor ear heard, have far more influence than any logical sequences whereby the same things may be demonstrated to the intellect.[6]

The author whose mind is infused with the Spirit of God captures truths that "dazzle gradually" through the story he is inspired to tell. For, being fallen as we are, the naked truth is "too bright for our infirm delight." The genius of the fairy tale is to present the reader with those moments of insight uniquely adapted to that reader's needs, and that unfold their insights by degrees as a person contemplates them.

When in the beginning of *Lilith* Vane the protagonist encounters the Raven, he asks where he is, and the Raven explains that he has come through a door. When Vane protests he is unaware of any door, he is told he has just come through a door "out"—that is, out of the physical world intellectually perceived—and finds himself "in"—that is, the world spiritually perceived by the heart. The Raven continues: ". . . the more doors you go out of, the farther you get in."

We confront a profound paradox. The doors "out" leave behind, not the physical world *per se*, but its appearances, that which the careless viewer mistakes for its realities. The doors "in" lead one to glimpses of higher reality, truths "too bright for our infirm delight." Such momentary perceptions—instances in which one loses a sense of self—come most often by indirection, and are perceived by the heart. They are mythic; they offer "a real though unfocussed gleam of divine truth falling on human imagination."[7] They exist quite beyond the reach of intellectual analysis and

> That frost of fact by which our wisdom gives
> Correctly stated death to all that lives.[8]

The worlds which an expert fantasist creates are conducive to such moments. MacDonald is such a genius.

The nature of fantasy is such that it allows for a range of interpretations. But the work of a dedicated Christian author, received by an earnest Christian reader—both being guided by the Spirit of God—offers deeply satisfying experiences of the truths that affect the human heart. This is another way of saying that what one sees in a work of art is a reflection of what a person is in one's innermost being. All art is like a mirror: it

---

6. Ibid., 419, 421.

7. Lewis, *Miracles*, chapter XV, n. 1.

8. Masefield, "Biography, II," in *Poems*, 267–68.

mirrors the quality of the mind of the creator, and the interpretation which any individual gives to it mirrors that person's state of being. Further, an author's sense of purpose has determined the imagery and the shape of the story, and all such choices are governed by the moral and spiritual quality of the author's mind. The more one knows about the life and thinking of an author, the more one understands why these particular choices were made and what his conscious purposes were.

The choices that a Christian author makes are controlled not only by that author's grasp of Christian truth, but also—and more importantly—by the degree to which that author has absorbed that truth in the very core of his being, so that it defines his life. From all that one can learn of George MacDonald's life, he was a fine model in this regard. An understanding of and a certain sympathy with his Christian convictions is necessary for a fuller appreciation of his work; this is true of the work of any sincere Christian author.

Symbolism vs. Allegory

A fairy tale is not an allegory. Its images are, rather, symbolic. Allegorical images and symbolic images are alike in that both mean themselves and something other than themselves. But in allegory there is no room for individual interpretation, as the "something other" is definitely indicated; in symbol, it is more indefinite and elusive, and is suggested by the context, so that interpretations may well vary. For instance, in John Bunyan's classic allegory *The Pilgrim's Progress,* no reader is in doubt as to the meaning of Mr. Worldly Wiseman or of Ignorance. However, in *At the Back of the North Wind,* a reader ponders the significance of North Wind, and of, say, the horse Diamond, and sees meanings unfold like a bud unfolds into a flower.

A good part of the fascinated bepuzzlement one feels in struggling to discern the meanings invested in MacDonald's fairy tales arises from the difficulties he faced when he undertook to convey his worldview while at the same time trying to avoid any trace of mechanical allegory. When near the end of his career he was writing and rewriting *Lilith* to get it precisely right, the publishing house G. P. Putnam's Sons of New York, who was preparing a new edition of his fairy tales, asked him for a preface, and in obliging them he made explicit his view of the nature of fairy tales and how they convey meaning. "A fairytale is not an allegory. There may be allegory in it, but it is not an allegory. He must be an artist indeed who can, in any mode, produce a strict allegory that is not a weariness to the spirit. An allegory must be Mastery or Moorditch."[9]

While refusing to offer a definition of the genre, he committed himself to say some things helpful to the reading of "such fairytales as I would wish to write, or care to read." He continued, "It cannot help having some meaning," but "one man will read one meaning in it, another will read another. . . . A genuine work of art must mean many things; the truer its art, the more things it will mean."[10] The imaginative reaches of such works invest them with a richness of implication, so that a range of interpretations is legitimate.

A basic reason why he emphasizes the multiplicity of meanings is that MacDonald felt strongly that each reader is at a different phase in that spiritual journey that all people are on, either progressing or retrogressing, according to how each is responding to whatever may be occurring in their lives. Wherever one is contributes strongly to the meaning that person sees in any of the events that befall, whether in real life or in imaginative stories. A basically good person sees a basically good world; an evil person an evil one.[11]

He therefore intends not to foist his own meanings upon the reader in any pedantic or arbitrary fashion: "The best thing you can do for your fellow," he concludes, "next to rousing his conscience, is—not to give him things to think about, but to wake things up that are in him; or say, to make him think things for himself." This caveat, then, gives us a solid clue as to how he is performing the very difficult task of not writing allegory but at the same time giving expression to his deepest convictions. He is giving his readers things to think about.

Anyone, therefore, who would undertake an explanation of any of MacDonald's fantasies would do well to keep in mind his strong denial that any given exposition is final. All that having been acknowledged, the temptation to share what one sees in them is strong, especially if one is convinced that each fantasy is a very worthy work of art, and that MacDonald's works do contain a great deal of truth. Such is the case with the present writer. Thus I am offering this reading.

George MacDonald was a deeply committed Christian and a worthy theologian. It is inevitable that his art be shaped by his deeply held

9. Hein, ed., *The Heart of George MacDonald*, 423.

10. Ibid., 425.

11. Cf. Ps 18:24–26.

theological convictions. My work is especially concerned to help the reader see the theological import of each fantasy.

Some of the meanings a given reader may glimpse may be deeply insightful and emotionally moving, quite beyond the ability of the mind to articulate. Such is the nature of Ultimate Reality, "too bright for our infirm delight," in Dickinson's fine phrase. J. R. R. Tolkien speaks of such moments as giving "a fleeting glimpse of Joy, Joy beyond the walls of the world, poignant as grief," and affirms that they may cause "a catch of the breath, a beat and lifting of the heart."[12] For many readers, MacDonald's works are redolent with images of this order.

When a given fantasy affords a reader fleeting glimpses into Ultimate Reality, it becomes mythic. The aura of myth is an atmosphere exuding Truth.

Receiving Myth

Like many words, the word *myth* can convey several meanings. I use it in the sense that J. R. R. Tolkien and C. S. Lewis gave to it. Christian myth is that species of imaginative writing that causes a catch of the breath, a faster beating of the heart, because it offers moments that arouse a deep-seated conviction that one has had a fleeting glimpse of eternal Reality. Such moments communicate something ineffable, quite beyond the reach of the intellect and its ability, beyond a point, to analyze.

These experiences will occur from different portions of a text, according to the nature and specific spiritual needs of any given reader. For instance, for me such moments have occurred in the scene in which Curdie is told to thrust his hands into a rose fire in *The Princess and Curdie*, or in the scene in Tolkien's *The Return of the Ring*, in which Sam awakes after being rescued and taken by an eagle into Gandalf's presence and hears Gandalf say, "A great Shadow has departed,' and then he laughed, and the sound was like music, or like water in a parched land." What is conveyed is something quite beyond the ability of the rational mind to articulate. One has a sudden, deep-seated conviction that one has a fleeting glimpse of Eternal Reality.

C. S. Lewis, much of whose thought is shaped by that of MacDonald, defines myth as "a particular kind of story which has a value in itself—a value independent of its embodiment in any literary work." Since he defines

12. Tolkien, "On Fairy Stories," *The Tolkien Reader*, 86.

myth in terms of its effect upon a person, he remarks, "it is plain that . . . the same story may be a myth to one man and not to another." But when a person encounters myth, "the experience is not only grave but awe-inspiring. We feel it to be numinous. It is as if something of great moment had been communicated to us."[13] He remarks that George MacDonald "is the greatest genius of this kind whom I know."[14]

It is the purpose of this work to explore several of George MacDonald's fantasies with a view to considering the themes and purposes that shape them. My hope is that readers will be helped to experience mythic moments and to receive "undefined, yet vivid visions of something beyond, something which eye has not seen nor heard."

Over the entirety of his career, MacDonald concentrated his attention upon the nature of the Christian life, insisting that its essence is imaginative obedience to the teachings of Jesus Christ, rather than simply embracing intellectually some rigorous doctrinaire position. Christian truths may seem dead and irrelevant to life unless they are imaginatively applied to experience. Each of the fantasies we consider here undertakes to explore imaginatively some aspects of this principle.

Phantastes is more comprehensive as it depicts the discovery of the riches of the world of spiritual reality. It is designed to free its readers from the narrow and circumscribed world of rational materialism and initiate them to the wealth of the spirit world, an orientation that leads into a full realization of what it means to be completely human. And *The Light Princess* affirms that the foundation for true spiritual experience is the sacrifice of Christ.

The Princess and the Goblin and *The Princess and Curdie* undertake to capture the charming nature of true encounters with and of an ongoing relation to the presence of God in individual lives, stressing the importance of obedience to the divine will and the help which it bestows upon the Christian worker. *At the Back of the North Wind* develops the principle announced at the conclusion of *Phantastes* and is a shaping influence in all the others, that is, that the presence of evil in the world carries with it the constant potential for good to be realized. The *Wise Woman* affirms the imperative for utter self-abnegation in the Christian life, and *The Golden Key* and *Lilith* explore with imaginative verve what experiencing of the world after death may be like.

13. Lewis, *An Experiment in Criticism*, chapter 5.
14. Lewis, *George MacDonald*, Preface.

It is the felt insights into the fuller dimensions of these basic Christian principles that give these fantasies their charm and guarantee their ongoing life.

1

Phantastes

"Will you take me for a pupil—a disciple—and teach me to believe—
or hope, if you like that word better—as you do?" Said Helen humbly.
How the heart of the curate beat—like the drum of a praising
orchestra!
"Dear Miss Lingard," he answered very solemnly, "I can teach
you nothing; I can but show you where I found what has changed
my life from a bleak November to a sunny June—with its thunder-
storms of doubt—but still June beside November. Perhaps I could
help you a little if you were really set out to find Jesus, but you must
yourself set out. It is you who must find him. Words of mine, as the
voice of one crying in the wilderness, may let you know that one is
near who thinks he sees him, but it is you who must search, and you
who must find." Thomas Wingfold, Curate, chapter XCVIII.

"I have had a great literary experience this week," C. S. Lewis exulted in a
letter to his friend Arthur Greeves in 1916 after he had purchased a copy
of *Phantastes*, and in subsequent letters there are many excited references
to it.[1] In an entry in his diary dated some seven years later he recorded: ". . .
I read Macdonald's *Phantastes* over my tea, which I have read many times
and which I really believe fills for me the place of a devotional book . . . ,"[2]
and in *The Great Divorce* he explained to MacDonald, when he met him in

1. Hooper, ed., *They Stand Together*, 92.
2. Ibid., 568.

the afterlife, that his "New Life" began when he first bought a copy.[3] The work has an intriguing ability not only to make the spiritual life attractive but also to draw a reader into it.

Phantastes is George MacDonald's first published adventure into adult fantasy, and *Lilith* his last. In *Phantastes,* we have his call to discover and enter into spiritual reality, together with his view of the nature of spiritual growth and becoming, views that he held consistently throughout his career and are foundational to all his writings. One must understand his thinking in order to enter into a better understanding of his rich contributions to the fairy tale genre. Anodos's adventures in Fairy Land show him as making these discoveries; Mr. Vane's experiences in *Lilith* show him as entering into the realm of Higher Reality beyond death; MacDonald hypothesizes that what has not been accomplished in these regards here must be there.

He saw in the religious world of his own day an excessive reliance upon reason together with an ignoring of the proper role of the imagination in entering into a vital relationship with God. In *Phantastes* he is endeavoring to show that the role of the imagination is critical in experiencing such a relationship. The mystical Land of Faerie becomes an elaborate metaphor for the realm of the supernatural, showing that rightly entering into and exploring the spiritual life is an adventure as exciting as dwelling in Fairy Land.

Chapters 1–3: Is There Such a Place as Fairy Land?

As *Phantastes* begins, the dominant theme is whether such a place as fairy land exists, and, if it does, what its nature is. Anodos's ignorance of this is representative of a mentality MacDonald saw strongly present in his time and that is predominant today, that is a set of mind that is convinced material reality encompasses all phenomena and the notion of spiritual reality is a chimera. Anodos's need is to forsake those constructions of reality he has inherited, which are severely inadequate, and come to an understanding of the true, whose values are defined at the conclusion of the tale. He is provoked to embark upon a metaphysical quest that leads him into a highly gratifying knowledge of the true nature of life.

As he rummages through his deceased father's papers, Anodos is confronted by "a tiny woman-form" who challenges his mild skepticism as to whether there exists somewhere a fairy country, and who promises that he

3. Lewis, *The Great Divorce,* chapter 9.

shall find his way into Fairy Land on the morrow. Gazing into her eyes fills him with "an unknown longing," and turning his attention to the view from his window in the moonlight, the engulfing fog that he sees seems at the same time to be an all-encompassing sea; such is the state of his mentality.

MacDonald's profound knowledge of Scripture shaped his imagination and permeated all his writings—not in the sense of literally quoting it, but in letting its spirit pervade his imagery. He may well have had in mind the writer of the Letter to the Hebrews saying "by faith we understand that the universe was created by the word of God, so that what is seen was not made out of things that are visible," and Paul's telling the Corinthian believers that "we look not to the things that are seen but the things that are unseen. For the things that are seen are transient, but the things that are unseen are eternal."[4] To enter Fairy Land is to encounter the conviction that the material world has a spiritual one within it; in Fairie "the whole of nature must be wondrously mixed with the whole spirit-world," to quote from Novalis's comment in the epigraph. Those who possess the sensibility to discern that richer reality and learn to be at home in it can come into a delightfully satisfying relation to life. It is an exciting adventure, answering to the "unknown longings" of the human heart.

Fairy Land is not simply a paradise; it is a world of great peril as well as exciting possibilities. As he awakes the following morning, Anodos finds his room transformed into an enchanting natural scene with a stream of water flowing through it. He washes in it, walks alongside it for a distance, then leaves it "without good reason, and with a vague feeling" that he ought to have followed its course. Although he takes "a more southerly direction" and enters "the darkest portion of the forest," he proceeds into Fairy Land by means of adventures uniquely appropriate to his personality and needs. His first encounter there is with a country maiden who stealthily tells him: "Trust the Oak, and the elm, and the great Beech. Take care of the Birch for though she is honest, she is too young not to be changeable. But shun the Ash and the Alder; for the Ash is an ogre . . . and the Alder will smother you with her web of hair, if you let her near you at night." Anodos needs help in discerning both the good and the evil: he needs to trust certain sources and shun others. His forthcoming adventures will teach him the reality of these sobering warnings.

Fairy Land is a place of learning the true nature of both good and evil, and the lessons Anados learns steadily contribute to his coming into

4. Heb 11:3; 2 Cor 4:18.

a more mature understanding of each. The name *Anodos* is derived from a Greek term which may mean either "having no way" or "rising." Both senses apply: he has no special purpose to follow in his life, and he makes some poor choices along the way, but, because of his positive attitudes and his determination to follow his curiosity, he grows in his knowledge and understanding of life. The vital knowledge that he acquires is given at the conclusion of the fantasy.

The concern at the threshold of Fairy Land is whether Anodos has "fairy blood," that is, the sensibility to participate in this higher world. As he wends his way, he comes upon a little cottage and asks for some food. The matron of the cottage tells him she sees that he has both a certain capacity and a need to feed upon the food of the land, but his education and thought processes have stifled that ability. The tragedy of living on the outskirts of Fairy Land but not having any interest in it and therefore effectively denying its existence is presented later in the form of her husband who, apparently, has not the requisite fairy blood.

Anodos accompanies the lady together with her daughter into their garden where they watch at length and with great pleasure the frolicsome activities of the fairies among the flowers, each flower having its distinct fairy. "The whole garden was like a carnival, with tiny, gaily decorated forms, in groups, assemblies, processions, pairs or trios, moving stately on, running about wildly, or sauntering hither or thither," Anodos observes. MacDonald is giving imaginative expression to his sacramental view of reality. Later, in his novel *Thomas Wingfold, Curate*, he gives it direct statement:

> . . . all about us, in earth and air, wherever eye or ear can reach there is a power ever breathing itself forth in signs, now in a daisy, now in a wind-waft, a cloud, a sunset; a power that holds constant and sweetest relation with the dark and silent world within us; that the same God who is in us, and upon whose tree we are the buds, if not yet the flowers, also is all about us—inside, the Spirit; outside the Word. And the two are ever trying to meet in us; and when they meet, then the sign without, and the longing within, become one in light, and the man no more walketh in darkness, but knoweth whither he goeth.[5]

The spirit present in each of the myriad forms of nature has the potential to communicate grace to all who have the eyes to see it. The proper

---

5. Chapter 82.

stance is keen observation, the effect, delight. "It seemed that intercourse with the fairies was no bad education in itself."

Chapter 4: A Story That Has No End

Bidding his hostess goodbye, Anodos journeys through the woods, fascinated by the various fairy presences he sees in the several flowers. On one occasion he overhears them gleefully saying: "Look at him! He has begun a story without a beginning, and it will never have any end." The individual is immortal; how a person interacts with this world of transcendent reality shapes one's life here and hereafter.

After a while the atmosphere changes. He begins to be haunted by feelings of fear and anxiety that some presence is approaching him, and he recalls the country maiden's warning concerning the Ash. With increasing terror Anodos flees through a drenching rain, stumbles and falls as a huge, grotesque hand hovers over him. But suddenly he is embraced by "soft arms" while a gentle feminine voice assures him he is safe with her. He finds himself at the base of a great tree, while the voice keeps murmuring, "I may love him, I may love him, for he is a man, and I am only a beech-tree." She is a tree, longing to be a woman, and in accord with an ancient prophecy, she is well on her way to becoming one. Anodos thinks her quite beautiful. Fairy Land has its mysteries, among them the inner relationship of humanity and the natural world.

They converse, she gives him a lock of her hair to protect him from further encounters with the Ash, and she warns the wood contains "more like me" from which the lock will offer no protection. Then she sweetly sings:

> I saw thee ne'er before;
> I see thee never more;
> But love, and help, and pain, beautiful one,
> Have made thee mine, till all my years are done.

He is enveloped with a euphoric feeling of well-being. Creating and communicating such moods is one of MacDonald's strengths. It is not only through expressions of love and assistance from others that one's spiritual life progresses, but also from its adversities, properly received. It would seem that in the realm of Faerie the workings of both good and evil are intensified.

Chapters 5–7: How Can Beauty and Ugliness Dwell So Near?

In his euphoric mood, Anodos begins to fantasize, shaping his own reality. Feeling a fascination for and a close affinity with this newly discovered world, he enters a rocky cell and sculpts from a block of marble a reposing woman, one that answers to the deepest longings of his heart. She is a palpable expression of his ideal, an incarnation of his "voiceless" longings. MacDonald is giving expression to that mysterious agitation in the depths of human consciousness that accounts for the ceaseless restlessness of mankind and motivates many individual pursuits. At the same time he is warning against devising ideals shaped by the lower aspects of one's nature, as opposed to receiving that which is given. As the form Anodos has shaped comes to life and "gleams" away through the woods, he is compelled to follow.

In pursuing her he encounters a forlorn knight whose apparel and demeanor bespeak his defeat in an unfortunate skirmish, and he warns Anodos concerning the Maiden of the Alder-tree. But confident in his own ability to avoid making any mistakes, Anodos shrugs off the warning and continues his pursuit. His surroundings become increasingly enchanting and he congratulates himself on the powers of his song that had awakened the lady. In a scene that steadily becomes more carnal, he hears her seductive voice, follows her into her grotto, and is mesmerized by her beauty. As Anodos is intent upon a night of love, she abruptly disappears and—in a scene that captures the horror of sudden, complete disillusionment—there stands in her stead the repugnance of an open coffin in the shape of a human body. As she scornfully laughs at him, he realizes that he has fallen prey to the Maid of the Alder and is confronted by the terrible truth that he has given himself "to a death of unfathomable horror." The Ash has overtaken him. But then he hears the dull sound of an axe and the Ash, feeling the blows, vanishes as quickly as it had appeared. Anodos is overwhelmed with chagrin.

This is the human dilemma: trying to realize one's ideal can so quickly become a self-centered pursuit for sensual gratification. Instead of being, as it should, a selfless pursuit, it can stealthily deteriorate into a self-aggrandizing quest that feeds one's pride and issues in a type of carnal satisfaction. The imagery very effectively captures the subtle and insidious ways in which one is oblivious to the manner in which the degeneration occurs.

The scene is echoing the biblical warning: "There is a way that seems right to a man, but its end is the way of death."[6]

As Anodos continues his journey, he ponders the enigma, "How can beauty and ugliness dwell so near?" That is indeed a mystery at the heart of life. Dostoevsky, MacDonald's contemporary, has Dimitri Karamazov crying similarly:

> "Beauty is a terrible and awful thing! . . . I can't endure the thought that a man of lofty mind and heart begins with the ideal of the Madonna and ends with the ideal of Sodom. . . . Is there beauty in Sodom? . . . Believe me, that for the immense mass of mankind beauty is found in Sodom. . . . The awful thing is that beauty is mysterious as well as terrible. God and the devil are fighting there and the battlefield is the heart of man."[7]

Dostoevsky's setting is realistic, MacDonald's fantastic; the emotional impact of the cry of both is powerful.

True to his name, Anodos proceeds he knows not whither and comes upon a farm house where he is welcomed by a kindly woman whose jovial but coarse-natured husband laughingly denies the very existence of Fairy Land. As he converses with Anodos their son enters and joins in the laughter, but his coarse sneering puts him in a different spiritual category from his father. Anodos spends a restful night with the family and in the morning departs with the son showing him a path which supposedly will avoid the house of the ogre, about whom Anodos has been warned.

Chapters 8–10: "Your Shadow Has Found You"

The warning against the ogre notwithstanding, Anodos leaves and comes upon a hut in which he hears a forbidding woman reading aloud a celebration of the eternity of darkness. Seeing a door in the corner, he opens it, and a shadow emerges from its far reaches, attaching itself to him.

He now becomes preoccupied with his shadow, and the result is that the enchanting charm in which he has beheld Fairy Land is no longer present. His world becomes common place and unattractive. Anodos's shadow is a spirit of analytical cynicism, a questioning, doubting attitude that is determined to "understand," dismissing imaginative perceptions as unreal

---

6. Prov 14:12.

7. *Brothers Karamazov*, book 3, chapter 3.

and fanciful. Common sense must "see through" them. It assumes that only that which can be rationally encompassed and explained is authentic. Mac-Donald is not opposing reason, but he felt strongly that reason must work in close accord with the imagination, obediently deferring to the latter's superior capacity to discern higher truth and reality.

That the shadow emerges from what we later learn is "the Church of Darkness" suggests this spirit is lethal to an effective and satisfying Christian life. Anodos meets the knight who had earlier warned him to beware the Maid of the Alder, and whose chopping had freed him from the Ash that had hovered over him. Formerly, the knight also had met the Maid of the Alder, but he had escaped by plunging into a "torrent of mighty deeds," thereby righting himself. In his writings MacDonald often emphasized that the key to avoiding such pitfalls in the Christian life is obedience to the divine precepts, actively pursuing courses of love.

Anodos must learn that truth painstakingly by a series of episodes. His shadow convinces him he should place confidence in his intellectual ability:

> In a land like this, with so many illusions everywhere, I need his aid to disenchant the things around me. He does away with all appearances, and shows me things in their true colour and form. And I am not one to be fooled with the vanities of the common crowd. I will not see beauty where there is none. I will dare to behold things as they are. And if I live in a waste instead of a paradise, I will live knowing where I live.

Such a rationalizing spirit privileges material reality to the extent of blinding itself to the spiritual essences resident in all things.

Possessed by this spirit, Anodos distrusts the very knight who would befriend him. He meets a little maiden who takes carefree pleasure in her little globe he destroys when he insists upon wrenching it from her; that is, he destroys her faith in her imagined world. He discovers that he must maintain a certain distance from people in order not to see them as grotesque. The landscape now becomes a rocky, sandy expanse, peopled with mocking goblins.

In his listlessness he comes upon a little stream, sips its water, and follows it as it gradually grows into a broad river on whose banks a lush verdure is flourishing. A spirit of joy returns and he feels as though he is "entering Fairy Land for the first time." Stepping into a little boat, he relaxes in an euphoric mood as he floats down the stream. This depiction of the water image, together with its several other very positive occurrences (it was by following a stream that he first entered into Fairy Land), is in harmony with its many biblical appearances, such as Christ's associating it with the new birth, or his dispensing the water of life to the Samaritan woman.[8]

Seeing the reflection of the moon in the waters, he reflects on the property of mirrors to enhance the loveliness of whatever they reflect.[9] His elated mood is intensified by his hearing the unique song of a bird, which, nevertheless, has a "tinge of sadness" in every note. He muses:

> Nor do we know how much of the pleasures even of life we owe to the intermingled sorrows. Joy cannot unfold the deepest truths, although deepest truth must be deepest joy. Cometh white-robed Sorrow, stooping and wan, and flingeth wide the doors she may not enter. Almost we linger with Sorrow for very love.

The depressed mood engendered by his experiences with his shadow is a prelude to fuller joy. Encounters with evil are somehow necessary for the realization of higher good.[10]

The stream carries him to the mythical fairy palace into which Anodos enters, is overcome by its elaborate charm, and follows its labyrinthine corridors until he comes upon a room whose door bears the inscription *The Chamber of Sir Anodos*. There he relaxes in surroundings uniquely designed for him and finds himself waited on by "invisible hands."

Chapters 11–13: "Who Lives, He Dies; Who Dies, He Is Alive"

In the morning Anodos awakens to a sense of belonging in an environs uniquely appropriated to his needs. Having progressed thus far in Fairy Land, he is discovering how his experience in it is now particularly fitted to his own individual necessities. A similar idea is stressed in *Lilith*. These works both emphasize the importance of a singular relation of the individual person to higher truth.

---

8. Cf. John 3:5; 4:14.

9. Page, ed., *Phantastes*, 15 observes: "*Phantastes* itself is a kind of magic mirror, through which we see life—our life—in a different way." In his writings MacDonald often affirms that mirror images hint at a higher reality.

10. This theme of the *felix culpa*, that evil functions in the creation of a greater good, comes to its fullest expression in *Lilith*.

Having achieved this state, Anodos finds that his shadow is barely discernible, and he is filled with the desire to be rid of it entirely: "Shadow of me . . . which art not me, but which representest thyself to me as me; here I may find a shadow of light which will devour thee." It seems banished for a time, only to reappear later.

Coming upon a huge basin of water hollowed out of the palace floor, he dives in, explores with fascination and delight rock formations he finds in the depths, and emerges refreshed. Having spent many days in this fashion, waited upon by invisible presences, he comes upon the palace library. Here day after day he envelops himself in the world of books, entering into the subject matter of each with such imaginative intensity that the world of the book becomes entirely his, and he the chief character in each recounted situation. MacDonald felt strongly that books can function sacramentally, conveying grace to those who enter their worlds with imaginative abandon. Scenes set in libraries often appear in his novels.

Chapter 12 begins with a remarkable statement on the unfathomable interrelationship of all things: "All that man sees has to do with man. Worlds cannot be without an intermundane relationship." And MacDonald's thought encompasses the hypothetical as well as the actual: "The blank, which is only a forgotten life, lying behind the consciousness, and the misty splendour, which is an undeveloped life, lying before it, may be full of mysterious revelations of other connexions with the worlds around us, than those of science and poetry." The discoveries of contemporary physics concerning the interrelatedness of all things come much nearer affirming MacDonald's vision than did the science of his day.

His vision encompasses much more than simply the material world; central to it is the richness of the unseen spiritual world. In the final chapters of *Lilith*, MacDonald returns to the idea in an attempt to realize the implications of this concept for the fully redeemed soul. In *Phantastes*, Anodos finds a book in the palace library that tells of a world in which this interrelationship is much more evident than in ours. Babies there are found by maidens in fully natural situations—"under an overhanging rock, or within a clump of bushes . . . or in any other sheltered and unexpected spot"—and the natural environs of the child determine its nature as a person.

Having entered imaginatively into this world, Anodos engages the inhabitants in conversation and, in response to their inquiries about how children are born in our world, he hints at the nature of human sexuality. Contemplating his explanation, one maiden is filled with an "indescribable longing" for death, and as is the practice in that land, retires to the place of her birth, and dies. This longing for death characterizes lovers, Anodos is told, and he feels that they must be reborn in our world, perhaps to find each other there.

The episode contains a fascinating ambiguity. Is MacDonald expressing a distaste for human sexuality? Or is he suggesting that the human manner of birth is superior to that found in this imagined realm, that lovers experience longings there that are not satisfied until they are born into another life in our world and perchance find each other? It would seem that, with typical Victorian restraint, he is suggesting the beauty and purpose of conjugal relationships.

However, he wants to emphasize an important caveat. The Cosmo story that follows further considers the nature of human love by underlining the fact that for one partner to attempt tyrannical control over the other is a sure way to destroy the value and beauty of the relationship. Cosmo is a poor student in ancient Prague who purchases a strange mirror from a musty armory shop, mounts it in his student lodgings, and is fascinated by the way its reflections transform the commonness of his room into something wonderful and fascinating. One evening as he gazes into the reflected room, a lovely woman of mournful countenance appears and reposes upon a couch. Existing as she does only in the mirror's reflection, Cosmo can only contemplate her beauty, and watching her as she returns each evening at the same time, he falls madly in love with her.

Determined to possess her, he casts a magic spell upon her and thus exercises "unlawful and tyrannical power." After he has brought her into his "veritable presence," he pleads his love for her. But his thus forcing her is destroying the possibility of their having a happy relationship. She confesses her love for him, but cries, "Cosmo, if thou lovest me, set me free." He struggles with his passion, for he now has her within his power, but, gaining the victory over his lower nature, he breaks the mirror, thereby setting her free.

But, alas, in breaking the mirror she disappears. Frantically hunting for her, he at last succeeds and is united with her, only to die as they embrace. The melodramatic tale has within it a statement of its moral: "Who lives, he dies, who dies, he is alive." For a marriage relationship to be healthy and happy, each individual must die to the self, destroying any inclinations to appropriate the mate for one's pleasure, and thus allow each to freely meet the partner as each chooses. True love cannot exist otherwise.

Chapters 14–18: Touch Not!

Delving more deeply yet into the mysteries of human consciousness, Anodos enters into the Hall of Phantasy; the text thus considers the ability of the mind to indulge through fantasy one's strongest desires. Here he conjures an image of his marble lady, and in a remarkably erotic song for the Victorian period, contemplates her beauty. Unable to restrain himself, he attempts to seize her, only to have her wrench herself free and flee with the reproach: "you should not have touched me." She disappears, and he finds himself in an "underground country" where, instead of trees and flowers, there is nothing but rocks and stones.

Anodos has experienced in his fantasizing what the Cosmo story should have sufficiently warned him against: to turn one's beloved into an object for one's selfish gratification, instead of honoring the mate's full personhood and individuality, is to destroy what otherwise could be a beautiful and fulfilling relationship. Restraint and purity of motive is necessary in the spiritual life as well as in the physical. The joy that Anodos had formerly experienced in the fairy castle was well within the bounds of moral restraint. Fantasizing activity is constantly tempting, but to violate the bounds of morality is not only to destroy joy, but also to land one in a spiritual wasteland.

In the destitute underground regions in which Anodos finds himself, hordes of demonic goblins mock him, some singing the song he had formerly sung to his marble lady. Among their jeering is the taunt: "You shan't have her; you shan't have her; he! he! She's for a better man; how he'll kiss her! How he'll kiss her!" Anodos passes a spiritual milestone when he retorts, "Well, if he is a better man, let him have her." The goblins are immediately foiled by his affirmation, turning their antics upon each other, and Anodos goes on his way singing. His song summarizes the moral lesson he has learned:

> In thy lady's gracious eyes
> Look not thou too long
> Else from them the glory flies,
> And thou dost her wrong.

> Come not thou too near the maid,
> Clasp her not too wild;
> Else the splendour is allayed,
> And thy heart beguiled.

Mac Donald is emphasizing that mature spiritual attitudes have strong implications for a person's sexual life.

Even so, Anodos is not beyond the reach of temptation. An elderly woman taunts him with the suggestion that he needs the accompaniment of a "pretty girl" to turn the drudgery of life into a pleasant affair, and then suddenly appears before him as a girl of ravishing beauty. But Anodos spurns her, thus confirming the moral commitment he has made.

His resolutions, however, are powerless to effect the freedom he desires. His former desires linger and he feels an ongoing pride in the power of his songs, together with certain regrets that he has indeed renounced his marble lady. Trudging onward through a gray mist, he finds himself beside a dismal and desolate sea, and he reaches the end of his endurance. Able to "bear it no longer," he resolves: "I will not be tortured to death. . . . I will meet it half-way. The life within me is yet enough to bear me up to the face of Death, and then I die unconquered." Arriving upon a low promontory, he gazes into "the heaving abyss," then plunges "headlong into the mounting wave below."

This action is pivotal; from it he emerges a changed being. Utterly renouncing the former self is a necessary spiritual prelude to his fuller joy, which immediately follows: "A blessing, like the kiss of a mother, seemed to alight on my soul; a calm, deeper than that which accompanies a hope deferred, bathed my spirit . . . ." The cold and stormy ocean is suddenly transformed into a peaceful summer sea and, gazing into its depths, he has pleasant visions of his "whole Past." Falling into a peaceful slumber, he now has "dreams of unspeakable joy."

His past experiences, sinful though some of them were, now all seem as a necessary prelude to this consummating and transforming spiritual experience. "I awoke with the feeling that I had been kissed and loved to my heart's content," Anodos affirms. From the fact that the listing of past personal events suggest some of MacDonald's own past is evidence that there is an autobiographical aspect to Anodos's adventures. In any case, here are echoes of MacDonald's conviction of the *felix culpa*, that good comes out of evil, a fallen world being its necessary context.

Chapter 19: "Live in the Love That Floweth Forth"

As a freshly born traveler, Anodos comes upon an island upon which there is no evidence of any other traveler, and on the island a cottage in which, entering, he finds an ancient woman figure who treats him as a loving mother. With a surge of happiness he bursts into tears, laying his head upon her bosom, and she feeds him like a baby.

In his writings MacDonald often refers to Christ's statement that, "unless you turn and become like children, you will never enter the kingdom of heaven,"[11] and Anodos is now as a freshly born child. Also, the figure of an ancient woman with a divine aura, which appears here and elsewhere in his fantasies, captures with the memorable impact of myth the gentle loving care of God bestowed upon those who come to him in full surrender. With Anodos reclining on a couch, the woman sits at his feet and sings him "The Ballad of Sir Aglovaile."

The ballad reiterates the theme of the Cosmo story, that restraint, self-control, and loving regard for the condition and desires of the beloved are essential for the health of a love relationship. The refrain is one of the most memorable of MacDonald's verses:

> Alas, how easily things go wrong!
> A sigh too much, or a kiss too long,
> And there follows a mist and a weeping rain,
> And life is never the same again.

Anodos now views his life in fresh perspective. The old woman's cottage has four sides, with a door in each. His hostess seems apprehensive as he approaches the door by which he had entered, and she advises him that he may return to her wherever he sees the dark red mark which she shows him upon the palm of her hand. As a stigmata it alludes to the sacrifice of Christ,[12] and the alert reader is reminded that it is only through Christ that we have free access to approach God.[13]

Anodos enters the door opening upon his past, and through it he recalls childhood scenes of his playing with his two brothers. The references seem to be to MacDonald's siblings with whom he was especially close: Alec, who died five years before the writing of *Phantastes,* and John, though still alive at the time of its writing, was to die a few months after.[14]

The scenes of childhood fill Anodos with grief and, returning to the old woman sitting at her spinning wheel, he hears her sing:

11. Matt. 18:4.

12. Page, ed., *Phantastes,* 209.

13. Cf. John 14:6.

14. For an exploration of the effect of Alec's death upon the text, see Page, ed., *Phantastes,* 21–22.

The great sun, benighted,
May faint from the sky;
But love, once uplighted,
Will never more die.

His courage returns, and he opens the door of Sighs.

Through the door of Sighs he is privileged to view unobserved his marble lady flying into the arms of "the knight of the soiled armour," whose armor now shines "like polished glass." He overhears their discussing his prior involvement in their lives, how he had freed her from an evil enchantment, and how in turn the knight had hewn the Ash tree and thus freed Anodos. The lady confesses she has love for Anodos still, but a greater love for her knight. Facing the test of being wrenched by disappointment and jealousy, Anodos in his mind affirms their love and pledges a subservient role in their lives; then, finding the mark, he returns to the ancient woman with her spinning wheel. There he bursts into a storm of tears, venting his pent-up emotion. The scene aptly recounts the inner emotional struggle involved in making noble decisions.

The woman at her spinning consoles him by emphasizing in song the moral beauty of self-sacrificing love, a theme which now becomes uppermost in Anodos's vision:

Better to sit at the waters' birth,
Than a sea of waves to win,

To live in the love that floweth forth,
Than the love that cometh in.

Be thy heart a well of love, my child,
Flowing, and free, and sure;
For a cistern of love, though undefiled,
Keeps not the spirit pure.

He now walks through the door of Dismay, and, in an enigmatic passage, he strolls through areas of "a great and solemn church," confronting other aspects of his past. Again, seeing the mark, he returns to "the ancient dame," hears her song that ratifies the past as somehow necessary to his present state: "The pangs of death are throbs of life." In spite of her warning previously given, he attempts to enter the final door—that of the Timeless—loses consciousness, and awakens in the ancient woman's lap as she weeps over him and lovingly restores him to life. Due to his disobedience, waters are rising around the cottage, but she has rescued him and now assures him that as long as she keeps her fire going, the threatening waters cannot enter her dwelling.

These last acts of disobedience and restoration obliquely suggest that the experiences of life, some of which may be ill-advised and wrong-headed, will finally yield good, if the doer duly returns to the divine presence. The woman counsels: "In whatever sorrow you may be, however inconsolable and irremediable it may appear, believe me that the old woman in the cottage, with the young eyes . . . knows something, though she must not always tell it, that would quite satisfy you about it, even in the worst moments of your distress." Divine grace constantly works to bring good out of evil. The scene foreshadows the final assurance that is announced at the conclusion of the fantasy.

The ancient woman now takes him by the hand and leads him through the door of Dismay, points out the direction he is to go, and commissions: "Go, my son, and do something worth doing." The scene neatly echoes Psalm 16:11: "You make known to me the path of life; in your presence there is fullness of joy; at your right hand are pleasures forevermore."

Chapters 20–21: Something Worth Doing

Obeying the ancient woman's directive, Anodos comes upon two brothers forging their swords in a "lonely tower." After receiving him warmly, they tell a tale of three giants who, after having restored an ancient castle nearby, were plundering the homes of the country people and kidnapping natives, demanding ransom. Attempts to defeat the giants have thus far failed.

The brothers relate to Anodos that an ancient wise woman had counseled them how to prepare to battle the giants, and had said she would find and send to them one "who will repay you well, in present song, and in future deeds." They engage Anodos to help and sing for them, which he does.

They engage the giants and are victorious, but at the cost of the lives of the two brothers. Anodos is the sole survivor. Exhilarated, he pridefully contemplates his victory, only to have his Shadow, absent for so long, reappear. Anodos undertakes to deliver the bodies of the brothers to their father, relates to him the details of the battle, and resumes his wanderings.

Chapter 22: The Slaying of the Self

This chapter memorably depicts the experience that MacDonald emphasizes is at the heart of the spiritual life: utter submission. Complete self-abnegation is necessary in order to enter into the proper relation to spiritual reality. The individual must be wary and the experience of self-abnegation renewed whenever pride arises. As Anodos proceeds, his "distressing" awareness of his Shadow's presence disappears as he contemplates himself in the company of the "glorious knights of old," on a par even with Sir Galahad. As he congratulates himself, he meets "a resplendent knight" in whom he sees his own image. But alas, the knight takes him captive, leads him to a dreary tower, and imprisons him there. Now he is alone and wretched, with a haunting conviction that his Shadow and the knight were one.

The atmosphere of his woeful and pathetic imprisonment is broken sporadically by the light of the moon shining through a hole in the roof, bringing a momentary feeling of release and joy. The scene portrays the tensions between the workings of divine providence, with the desires it arouses in him through his dreams, and the inner dismal vacuity of the prideful self. Then, after he hears a woman singing of how the rays of the sun liberate the natural world, he opens the prison door and walks freely out into the welcoming world. Why had he not done so before? he asks.

Anodos now meets the woman whose song has set him free and learns that she is the one whose globe he formerly broke. She thanks him for the experience, for her sorrow taught her to sing, and her songs not only give her pleasure, but also help others, as she has just helped him. Anodos muses: "She was uplifted, by sorrow and well-doing, into a region I could hardly hope ever to enter." As he leaves her, he hears her singing:

> Thou goest thine, and I go mine—
> Many ways we wend;
> Many days, and many ways,
> Ending in one end.
>
> Many a wrong, and its curing song;
> Many a road, and many an inn,
> Room to roam, but only one home
> For all the world to win.

So the mysterious and inscrutable workings of providence will eventually realize final good for all.

The more immediate lesson, however, that Anodos has repeatedly learned, is "the delight of being lowly; of saying to myself, 'I am what I am, nothing more.' I learned that he that will be a hero, will barely be a man; that he that will be nothing but a doer of his work, is sure of his manhood." In no longer aspiring to knighthood he has lost his shadow. He also perceives that to contemplate his newly gained humility is to lose it: "Self will come to life even in the slaying of self." So self-denial must be regularly reaffirmed.

Chapter 23: Great Men Made of Wood

Proceeding, Anodos meets the knight "of the soiled armour" returning from a skirmish, and pledges himself to serve the knight as his squire.[15] The knight relates an account of how he had rescued a little girl who was gathering butterfly wings which would enable her to fly away, but who was harassed and prevented by rogues—"great men, made of wood, without knee or elbow-joints, and without any noses or mouths or eyes in their faces." In fighting with them, the knight discovers he can subdue them by tripping them up and setting them upon their heads.

As Anodos and his knight ride deeply into the forest, they come upon a vast clearing in which a crowd of worshipers are in rapt attention. The knight partakes of the worshipful attitudes of the crowd, but Anodos is increasingly suspicious of the event, convinced there was evil at its heart. Disguising himself in a white robe like the worshipers, he mounts the throne, and hurls the great wooden image from off its throne. Thus uncovering a great hole in the throne, a great wolf-like brute emerges with which Anodos fiercely struggles. Overwhelmed by the rushing crowd of devotees, he is slain.

The scene is strongly autobiographical, revealing how at this juncture in his life MacDonald viewed the ministry into which he was feeling called. He saw within the churches at large a prevailing spirit and set of mind that was inimical to the true spirit of the gospel, which presents the all-encompassing love of God as Father and strongly calls people into experiencing his tender mercies, taking up a cross, and following Christ in full obedience to his precepts. Usurping the churches, "great men made of wood" were—in their hypocritical assumptions of self-righteousness—terribly misleading earnest seekers who, like the little girl trying to gather wings

---

15. The knight may be a surrogate for Alexander Scott, a deposed Presbyterian minister whose teachings MacDonald much admired.

from butterflies and moths, desired simple help in understanding the true gospel. These false teachers represent God more as a fearsome tyrant than a loving father. To set them "upon their heads" by proclaiming divine truths as he understood them was MacDonald's strong calling, evident throughout his sermons and novels.

Chapter 24: Content in a Coffin

Momentarily Anodos has a vision of being dead. As he reposes in his coffin, the knight and his lady mourn his passing and celebrate his achievements. He is in full blessedness, and he comprehends the central truths about life. He now understands that:

> . . . it is by loving, and not by being loved, that one can come nearest the soul of another; yea, that where two love, it is the loving of each other, and not the being loved by each other, that originates and perfects and assures their blessedness. I know that love gives to him that loveth, power over any soul beloved, even if that soul know him not, bringing him inwardly close to that spirit; a power that cannot be but for good; for in proportion as selfishness intrudes, that love ceases, and the power which springs therefore dies. Yet all love will, one day, meet with its return. All true love will, one day, behold its own image in the eyes of the beloved, and be humbly glad.

Juxtaposed against this central truth is a vision of the hopeless squalor of slum dwellings, and he pledges himself to a ministry of working with needy peoples when he returns to his earthly life.

Chapter 25: Something too Good to be Told

The vision of Fairy Land concluded, Anodos is back at his ancestral home, authority over which he must now assume. His just having arrived at his twenty-first birthday has brought him to physical and legal maturity, and his now having traveled through Fairy Land, with its full orientation to spiritual reality, has brought him to spiritual maturity. The challenge is now before him to effectively apply the truths he has learned to everyday life.

He is filled with joy to discover that the pledge he has made to live a life of loving ministry to his fellow men has freed him from the presence of his Shadow. Whenever he is struck by the suggestion that his vision of the higher reality of Fairy Land seems to him to be too good to be true, he recalls the wise woman of the cottage and her "solemn assurance" that she knew something "too good to be told." The perplexities of this life are equivalent to his having passed through the Door of Dismay, and the way back is through his tomb.

Anodos ends his story by recounting a vision he had while on a noon break from working in the fields with his reapers. Lying in the cooling shade of a beech tree, he seemed to hear the ancient woman's singing, "A great good is coming—is coming to thee, Anodos," and he was filled with quiet joy at that assurance. Though her voice faded, he now confidently affirms: ". . . I know that good is coming to me—that good is always coming; though few have at all times the simplicity and the courage to believe it. What we call evil, is the only and best shape, which, for the person and his condition at the time, could be assumed by the best good."

This affirmation, made near the beginning of his long ministry, is central to the entirety of George MacDonald's thought as he expressed it in his many fairy stories, his series of *Unspoken Sermons*, and his novels. Whenever someone would remark that what he held was "too good to be true," he was fond of replying, "It's so good it has to be true."

To know the totality of MacDonald's thought and the seriousness with which he treats any deviation from moral rectitude is to know this is not a hopelessly Pollyannaish vision. He saw it as quite in line with a mature understanding of biblical teaching.

2

The Light Princess

The life of Christ is this—negatively, that he does nothing, cares for nothing for his own sake; positively, that he cares with his whole soul for the will, the pleasure of his father. Because his father is his father, therefore he will be his child. The truth in Jesus is his relation to his father; the righteousness of Jesus is his fulfilment of that relation. Meeting this relation, loving his father with his whole being, he is not merely alive as born of God; but, giving himself with perfect will to God, choosing to die to himself and live to God, he therein creates in himself a new and higher life; and, standing upon himself, has gained the power to awake life, the divine shadow of his own, in the hearts of us his brothers and sisters, who have come from the same birth-home as himself, namely, the heart of his God and our God, his father and our father, but who, without our elder brother to do it first, would never have chosen that self-abjuration which is life, never have become alive like him. To will, not from self, but with the Eternal, is to live. "Creation in Christ," *Unspoken Sermons, Series Three.*

*P*hantastes, which was published in 1858, was not well received, and MacDonald tried his hand at writing novels. That George Eliot's early novels were being very well received suggested to him how the author's voice attractively presented could comment extensively upon life. He wrote the novel *David Elginbrod*, in which he managed to express an appreciable quantity of Christian truth. It is modeled upon the life of his father whom he had greatly admired and saw as an ideal Christian. After a considerable struggle to get it published, it appeared in 1863 and was very well received. MacDonald was launched on his extensive novel-writing career. He was strongly convinced, however, that fairy tales had an imaginative appeal that novels lacked and could explore truths in a manner that realist novels could not. Eternal truths were often too elusive to be captured by reasoned exposition. Fairy tales were the more effective genre in communicating these. But how could he entice a larger audience to read them? Perhaps he could combine the two genres to better fulfil his purposes.

In 1864 he published *Adela Cathcart*, a work that seeks to do just that. The plot is meager: the young Adela is gripped with a malaise that has baffled the doctors and seems to have no physical cause or available cure. Convinced that her problem is one of spirit rather than body, friends begin telling her fairy tales, and they indeed restore her to full health. Each of the tales has a theme which conveys a spiritual impact. The most thematically significant is *The Light Princess*, which affirms through parable-like imagery that the basis for Christian experience is the sacrifice of Christ.

The captivating opening of this tale cannot but engage the imagination, and the humor throughout, with its frequent punning and wordplay, establishes an engaging tone. After long waiting, a king and his queen finally have a child: a little girl. The king invites many guests to the christening but, alas, neglects to ask his sister, Princess Makemnoit. Outraged, the offended princess appears anyway and, having the powers of a witch, manages to cast a spell upon the child that deprives her of her gravity. This results in the little princess floating upwards and hovers near the ceiling whenever she is unrestrained. The playful use of the term *gravity* is made to have strong spiritual implications. Suggesting as it does a mature and somber tone, it is a characteristic of spiritual health. Deprived of it, the princess reacts to all aspects of life with an unrestrained hilarity, causing her parents and all who tend her dismay and distress. Mature and sober attitudes in life are thus made to appear very desirable without the narrating voice making direct didactic statements to this effect.

Frantic to find a remedy to correct his daughter's condition, the king consults the materialist Hum-Drum and the spiritualist Kopy Keck. Their diagnoses and remedies are both wide of the mark and ludicrous. Thus MacDonald holds up to ridicule the increasingly popular contemporary analyses of the human condition he sees offered by the materialists and psychologists of his day. The tale presents water imagery to emphasize many aspects of the true life of the spirit, thereby making subtle reference to the biblical uses of water. In Scripture it often symbolizes access to true spiritual life. For example, it is necessary for baptism, and Christ presents himself as the water of life. Near the palace is a beautiful lake that the princess loves. When she swims in it, she finds her gravity restored and is amazed to feel true pleasure—instead of her hollow fits of laughter. Not only so, but she is more beautiful, modest, and maidenly when she is enjoying a swim in its waters.

As one expects in a fairy tale, a handsome prince appears. He joins the princess in her nightly swims and soon falls in love with her in the water. He is "fine, handsome, brave, generous, well-bred, and well-behaved, as all princes are," we are told. The use of prince and princess imagery suggests impeccable moral character.

But alas, the water level begins to ebb. When the princess discovers that the lake is receding, she is in great distress. In a delightfully vivid passage MacDonald details how the wicked witch had gained access through her underground passages to the underside of the lake, and by employing the services of the White Snake of Darkness, had effected a hole whereby the water began to drain away. She also by means of her hexes dried all the mountain streams that fed the lake. Soon all of the lake that remains is a basin in the center that contains the remnants of the water. The princess becomes morose and emaciated as though, we are told, the lake were her soul. A solution is found when a neighborhood lad peers into the basin and discerns at its bottom a plate of gold that on one side bears the words:

> Death alone from death can save.
> Love is death, and so is brave
> Love can fill the deepest grave
> Love loves on beneath the wave

Writing on the reverse side explains that only the body of a living man can stop the escaping waters, and he must die in the process. The prince offers so to sacrifice himself. He finds the leak and plugs it with his body, even though the princess is bored and indifferent while the waters slowly rise to engulf him. All this is, of course, a cleverly disguised presentation of the Christian gospel. MacDonald is here supplying what *Phantastes* lacked: any specific reference to the death of Christ. In *Phantastes* Anodos commits suicide by plunging into the sea and is reborn, and he is shown as learning in death the nature and importance of a life of love, but the reason why such dying is effective is not given. Here it is made quite clear. Human souls are doomed without the efficacy of a sacrifice on their behalf; in joining in the sacrifice of Christ they are set free.

The calloused indifference that the princess offers as regards the self-giving of the prince reflects something of the attitudes of many outwardly confessing Christians to the crucifixion. In nurturing him with wine and a biscuit, however, the princess "was compelled to look at him," just as in partaking of the Eucharist communicants are forced to give their attention to Christ's sacrifice.

"Love and water" thus restores the princess to full health. Although the prince is inundated with water and apparently has drowned, the princess desperately extracts him from the lake and has him taken to her room where he is resurrected. The princess now finds she cannot walk until she comes to terms with gravity, which, with the prince's loving help, she does. Thus the tale ends with the suggestion that with Christ's help a person can acquire that set of mature and sober attitudes towards life that render it truly meaningful.

3

The Princess and the Goblin

Brothers, have you found our king? There he is, kissing little children and saying they are like God. There he is at table with the head of a fisherman lying on his bosom, and somewhat heavy at heart that even he, the beloved disciple, cannot yet understand him well. . . . The God who is ever uttering himself in the changeful profusions of nature; who takes millions of years to form a soul that shall understand him and be blessed; who never needs to be, and never is, in haste; who welcomes the simplest thought of truth or beauty as the return for seed he has sown. . . . the God of music, of painting, of building, the Lord of Hosts, the God of mountains and oceans; whose laws go forth from one unseen point of wisdom . . . the God of history working in time unto Christianity; this God is the God of little children, and he alone can be perfectly, abandonedly simple and devoted. The deepest, purest love of a woman has its well-spring in him. "The Child in the Midst," *Unspoken Sermons: Series One.*

G. K. Chesterton wrote:

. . . I for one can really testify to a book that has made a difference to my whole existence, which helped me to see things in a certain way from the start; a vision of things which even so real a revolution as a change of religious allegiance has substantially only crowned and confirmed. Of all the stories I have read, including even all the novels of the same novelist, it remains the most real, the most realistic, in the exact sense of the phrase the most

like life. It is called *The Princes and the Goblin,* and is by George
MacDonald . . . .[1]

A fantasy, the "most real . . . the most like life"? Quite evidently this
fantasy had communicated to Chesterton as a child something ineffable
about the nature and significance of life, insights that no realistic literature
had. It had functioned as only pure myth can.

MacDonald published this tale in 1872, after his reputation as a
successful novelist and writer of fairy tales was well established. Having
depicted the spiritual life in *Phantastes* as an exciting and soul-satisfying
adventure of discovery, he turns in this tale to explore the true nature of
God and of a proper relationship to him. He dares to use the image of a
great-great-grandmother for the Divine Presence, an image that serves
him well in communicating both God's loving concern and his seeming
capriciousness.

The Princess Loses Herself: Chapters 1–5

The story begins by describing a little princess named Irene[2] who lives, not
with her father in his grand and beautiful castle in the mountains, but with
"some country people" in a "large house, half castle, half farmhouse, on the
side of another mountain." In the subterranean regions of the mountain
live a race of grotesque goblins that delight in emerging to torment people.

One day the princess is wandering through her strange home and
comes upon a series of stairs. Climbing them, she finds a room in which
she espies a very old and very beautiful lady spinning on a spinning wheel.
When the lady engages her in conversation, she learns their names are the
same, Irene, and that she is her great-great-grandmother.

Metaphorically, the situation may be understood to suggest the human psyche presented in Pauline terms, with the goblins representing
what Paul calls "the flesh," or the "old man"—our sinful nature—while the
great-great-grandmother depicts the Divine Presence, which can be visited
within if, like Irene, one has lost one's self, and climbs high enough.[3] That

1. Greville MacDonald, *George MacDonald and His Wife,* 9.

2. MacDonald's fifth child, born August 31, 1857, was named Irene. She must have
been delighted to have her father writing about another Irene.

3. The principle stated in Revelation 3:20 is suggested: "Behold, I stand at the door
and knock. If anyone hears my voice and opens the door, I will come in to him and eat
with him and he with me."

the names are identical graphically captures the truth that in God "we live and move and have our being," as Paul told the Athenians.[4]

C. S. Lewis speaks of the fairy tale as that form best suited for what he had to say.[5] For George MacDonald it was the only way he could successfully and without offense introduce such a radically different depiction of God. He was deeply convinced that the prevalent descriptions of God in his day were exclusively intellectual and abstract, creating the impression that God was like an all-powerful dictator on a remote throne, coldly demanding the fulfillment of his desires. MacDonald wanted people to see God rather as tender-hearted and lovingly concerned for his children, helping them obey that which was for their good. The image of an ancient, loving grandmother, beckoning to people, tenderly ministering to their needs, and helping them obey, serves his strongly held theological convictions well.

There is yet further way in which the maternal image is apt. All are born of woman—the life of all species comes through the female. People are individually created by God, and it is by meeting God within that they are born again and receive life from above. Humanity has its origin in God; he created us, as MacDonald remarks in one of the novels, out of "his own endless glory." All life is from him.

People who submit to God in repentance and faith often can point to a specific time when their spiritual eyes were opened. The imaginative experience that the reader has in the scene of Irene meeting her great-great-grandmother may well be one of those moments that prompt a catching of one's breath and a sense of joy. Wordsworth declares:

> There are in our existence spots of time
> That with distinct pre-eminence retain
> A renovating virtue.[6]

Such moments are mythic. MacDonald's fantasies are capable of presenting the attentive reader with many.

One of the charms of MacDonald's fantasies is the winsome manner in which he gives disguised expression to theological truths. Excited by her delightful adventure, Irene runs to tell her nurse, and is deeply hurt when she discovers the nurse does not believe her story, but thinks she has been dreaming. But the princess pertly replies: "No, I didn't dream it. I went

---

4. Acts 17:28.

5. Hooper, ed., *The Letters of C. S. Lewis*, 587.

6. *The Prelude*, bk. XII, in Gill, ed., *William Wordsworth*.

upstairs, and I lost myself, and if I hadn't found the beautiful lady, I should never have found myself." It is in a right relationship to the Divine Presence that a person's true humanity begins to develop.

Another example occurs in the next chapter, in which the Princess again sets off to encounter her great-great-grandmother and is unable to find the stairs that take her there. Momentarily she doubts the reality of her past experience; perhaps it was a dream after all. At least, "she thought it very sad not to have been able to find her when she particularly wanted her." One cannot command epiphanies at will; they come at the behest of the Divine Presence alone, not ours.

Adventures in the Mines: Chapters 6–9

On a delightful, sunshiny day, Irene and her nurse go out for a walk and get lost on the mountain, having gone too far. When goblins peering from hidden places begin taunting them, they suddenly meet a boy coming up the mountain singing. He is Curdie, a miner's son. He explains that his songs fill the goblins with fear and keep them at bay. An upbeat, positive, and caring attitude is an effective deterrent to assaults from one's lower nature.

When Curdie leads them safely back to their home, Irene attempts to give him the kiss she has promised for extricating them from their dilemma. Lootie the nurse, however, adamantly prevents her, and Irene is dismayed not to be able to keep her promise. Curdie resolves the issue by excusing himself and vowing to come another time. Lootie now has a double charge: keeping Irene from the goblins, and from Curdie, a mere miner's son.

Curdie works with his father in the mines deep underground. One night, working alone, he overhears a conversation among the goblins, and learns that though their heads are quite hard, their feet are soft and vulnerable, and that they are planning an attack upon the palace.

After the goblin family whose conversation he has overheard departs, Curdie, discovering some loose stones in the wall, hurriedly burrows through into their quarters, and stealthily follows them as they make their way to the goblin palace. When they arrive, Curdie surreptitiously views in awe a horde of goblins gathered before the king and his court in a magnificent cavern, and overhears their devious plans.

After being convinced that a part of the goblins' scheme is to destroy the mines by breaking outlets for the water that was held in the mountain's natural reservoirs and thus inundating them, Curdie finds his way back through the dark tunnels. He carefully fills up the hole through which he had come and leaves for his home, telling his father what he has learned.

Curdie spends many nights alone in the mine, working for a time, then exploring the goblins' tunnels. He always finds his way back successfully by using a ball of string, tying one end to his stationary pick-axe, unwinding the ball as he proceeds, and carefully following the thread back to his destination, winding it back into a ball as he goes.

While Curdie is thus exploring, strange grotesque creatures, like deformed animals, are spotted at night gamboling around the palace grounds. They are "household animals belonging to the goblins"; some have grown "in grotesque resemblance to the human." In MacDonald's fantasy world, there are a multitude of creatures either devolving in various stages down from the human through the animal kingdom, or else evolving through successive stages toward the higher human. Attitudes and accompanying actions, good or bad, determine which.

Irene's Further Visits: Chapters 10–11; 14–17

Irene is thrilled to have her father the King visit her, coming in all his royal pomp. When she excitedly asks him to visit her old grandmother, he is skeptical, and has a reprimanding talk with Lootie. One night Irene, thinking she may be dreaming, again finds her way up the back stairs and into the mysterious old lady's presence. When Irene asks why she could not find her before, the lady replies, "you would have found me sooner if you hadn't come to think I was a dream." She instructs the princess not to say anything more to Lootie about her because she is not able to believe. Shades of the doctrine of election are here.

In a scene fraught with mythic suggestions, the old lady tells Irene she is spinning a very thin thread for her; she then applies fragrant ointment to Irene's hand that she had accidently pricked with a brooch, shows her to her bedroom, and asks if she would like to sleep with her. When the princess asks if the lady will extinguish the moon, she is told, were she to do so, "you would fancy yourself lying in a bare garret, on a heap of old straw, and would not see one of the pleasant things round about you all the time." The moon in MacDonald's fantasies is a persistent symbol of the providential presence of God. Its benign presence is constant, not predestinating events, but persistently shining a dim light upon the way one should choose. Before the night is over, the grandmother gives Irene a behest to obey: she must be certain to return to her "this night week," and she must not think it all a dream.

Irene impatiently awaits the night upon which she is to return to her old grandmother, but when it arrives, she is suddenly startled by the intrusion of a grotesque, cat-like creature. Gripped with fear, instead of climbing the stairs as she should have, she runs out onto the mountain in the dark. Momentarily lost, she espies the rising moon, which she recognizes as her great-great-grandmother's lamp, and she follows its light to return her to her palace. She hurriedly climbs the stairs and knocks at the old lady's door.

After being graciously received by the beautiful grandmother and being assured that, in spite of her frightened fleeing to the mountain, she has done nothing wrong, Irene is delighted with the strange rose-fire in the hearth and the beauty of "sky, moon, and stars" in the old lady's bath. When Irene asks about the light in the sky that showed her the way back to the castle, she is told that not everybody is able to see it, though she hopes some day everybody will. Before Irene leaves, the grandmother presents her with a trial: she must return on this night one week later, and must not feel she has had but a dream.

The grandmother presents Irene with a present she has been preparing for her: a ball spun of thread so fine no one can see it. She ties one end to a small ring that is on the princess' hand, and then she tells her that, if ever she finds herself in any danger, she is to place the ring under her pillow, and then place her finger upon the thread and follow it wherever it may lead. Had Irene dismissed her first visit with her great-great-grandmother as a dream, she would of course not have had the second visit nor be entrusted with the special task that lies ahead.

So both Curdie and Irene have balls of string or thread. There is, however, a large difference. Irene's is given her by God; Curdie's string is his own devising, and has a different outcome. Through charming indirection MacDonald is showing that if a person has a relationship to God filled with trust and earnest obedience, the path of life will be shown one. MacDonald may well have been inspired to use the ball and thread imagery by finding it in a poem by a favorite poet of his, William Blake. Blake wrote:

> I give you the end of a golden string
> Only wind it into a ball:
> It will lead you in at Heaven's gate,
> Built in Jerusalem's wall.[7]

7. *Jerusalem*, chapter 3, plate 77, in Johnson and Grant, eds., *Blake's Poetry and*

The strings play a crucial part in the narrative.

Curdie in Trouble: Chapters 12–13; 18–19

When Curdie, on one of his nocturnal adventures, begins to return following his string, he is dismayed to find it leading him through unfamiliar places. The goblins had discovered and moved his pick axe. Groping through the dark, he comes upon an assembly of goblins and stealthily overhears them. But inadvertently he slides into their midst, arousing them to fight. He makes a valiant effort to defend himself but is finally overcome and imprisoned. He is defeated by the queen who, because of the embarrassment she feels over having deformed feet, wears granite shoes. Having disabled Curdie by stamping on his foot, she throws him into a hole in the wall. But in his cell Curdie overhears his captors argue whether to starve him for a while before they kill him, or rather to fatten him and feed him as a treat to their animals.

Curdie's string has gotten him into deep trouble.

Following the Thread: Chapters 20–21

Meanwhile, Irene awakens to feel the tug of her thread, and, following it, she is surprised to have it lead her, not up the stairs to her grandmother's, but rather out along the mountainside, up its rough ascent, and through a hole into the darkness of its interior. Buoyed by thoughts of her grandmother's kindness, she follows the thread by faith down rough stairs and through a maze of narrow passageways, only to find it disappears into a pile of stones. Feeling herself forsaken, she bursts into wailing. Then, it occurs to her to remove stones so she could continue following the thread, and doing so, she finds herself after much diligent work in Curdie's presence.

Curdie's puzzlement as to who Irene is and how she got there is superceded by his desire to escape, but, after clearing away the stones and a slab, they disagree as to how to proceed. Curdie yields to Irene's insistence that they must follow the thread even though he is convinced it is leading them the wrong way, and they come upon the goblin king and queen asleep on their sheepskin bed. Convinced that if he could extract the sleeping queen's

---

Designs.

shoes he would no longer need to be afraid of them, he does so, revealing the queen's deformed six-toed foot, but waking the royal pair in the process.

They escape by fleeing through the darkness. Irene keeps insisting they must carefully follow wherever the thread leads them, although Curdie thinks her tale of her grandmother is nonsense. When she asks him to feel the thread for himself, he feels nothing at all. It leads them into a stream of water, and following it they emerge in Irene's own garden. As the string leads them into the house and up the stairs toward the grandmother, Irene urges Curdie to continue with her and make the grandmother's acquaintance.

The central theme of *The Princess and Curdie* can be seen to be beautifully stated in Proverbs 3:5,6: "Trust in the Lord with all your heart, and do not lean on your own understanding. In all your ways acknowledge him, and he will make straight your paths." Curdie followed his own understanding—symbolized by his following his string—and, noble though his purposes were, he fell into deep trouble. In contrast, Irene's string led them both to safety because it was followed by faith in its divine source, even though at times it defied their own calculations.

The Old Lady and Curdie: Chapter 22

To Irene's dismay, Curdie is utterly unable to see the grandmother who receives her so warmly. In contrast to Irene's interaction with her, Curdie sees only a bare garret with "a tub, and a heap of musty straw, and a withered apple, and a ray of sunlight coming through a hole in the middle of the roof." The old lady explains to Irene: "You must give him time and you must be content not to be believed for a while. It is hard to bear, but I have had to bear it." When Irene asks what it all means, she is told: "It means . . . that I did not mean to show myself. Curdie is not yet able to believe some things. . . . you must be content . . . to be misunderstood for a while. . . . But there is one thing much more necessary. . . ," that is, "to understand other people."

Curdie thanks Irene for rescuing him, but leaves in a huff, thinking she has made a fool of him in the end. The Grandmother lovingly ministers to Irene, bathing her in a "large silver bath," while she sings her a "strange sweet song" whose sense transcends understanding, but gives her deep joy.

There is much of MacDonald's theology here. All people are on a spiritual continuum, as it were, either making progress by their attitudes and decisions towards purity of heart and a believing, trusting, relationship to God, or they are retrogressing, by way of submission to evil, "going downhill towards the animal country," i.e., gradually diminishing their humanity. Curdie, in his earnestness to do good and defeat evil, is spiritually developing in the right direction, but he has not yet come to that state in which he is "able to believe." However, the grandmother is not through with Curdie.

Disgusted and confused, Curdie tells his mother of his frustration, and she remarks that" some people can see things other people can't see." She then relates to him how as she was returning to her home one night alone on the mountain, she was attacked by a group of cobs. Suddenly, as they tore upon her, a light shone from above and a white dove descended upon its beam. Frightened, the cobs fled, and she returned safely to her home. His mother's experience leaves Curdie more open to believe Irene and he wishes to serve her. However, because he is but a miner's son and she a princess, he has no free access to her.

The Goblins in the King's House: Chapters 23–27

While Curdie was in the mine and stealthily overhearing the goblins' conversations, he was convinced they have a plot to capture the Princess Irene and give her in marriage to Harelip, their prince, and thereby use her as a hostage to gain control over the castle. Curdie returns briefly to the mine and confirms his suspicions that the goblins are indeed burrowing towards the castle. Wanting to keep track of the goblins' tunneling movements, Curdie stealthily visits at night the gardens of the castle to see if he can detect any evidence of their approach. One night the guards see him and, thinking he is one of the goblin's creatures, shoot and wound him with a crossbow. Captured, he is kept by the soldiers in a room of the castle, where he moves in and out of delirium. In moments of clarity he tries to warn them of the threatening danger, without success.

Meanwhile, the goblin horde succeed in arriving under the castle floor and break through into the castle. On that very night Curdie—while in delirium—is visited by a white-haired old lady who heals his wound and restores him to health. Hearing the commotion below stairs, he rushes into the midst of the guards battling the goblins; he stamps on their feet while he sings his hastily conceived rhymes. When the goblins are finally driven out of the castle, Curdie rushes to Irene's room to find it empty.

The Promised Kiss: Chapters 28–32

As soon as Curdie determines to rescue the princess as she had rescued him, he feels a slight touch on his hand and, reaching, feels a thin thread. Thinking it must be the same thread the princess used in rescuing him, he follows it. To his surprise, it leads him up the mountainside to his parents' home, and there he finds the princess in the comforting arms of his mother. The princess Irene tells him how she had awakened to find the thread, and following it, was led up mountain to this destination. As they ponder the circumstances that have brought them safely together, Curdie is becoming convinced of the reality of Irene's old grandmother.

Suddenly remembering how he had overheard the goblins' scheme to flood the mine, Curdie dashes off to warn his father of the impending disaster. He finds the miners working feverishly to fortify the walls of the mine against the possibility of its being flooded. He and his father then return to their cottage. A raging storm arises, preventing their returning the princess to her home that evening, so they rest until the morning.

The following morning Curdie and his mother return the princess to her home and find her king father has arrived. Amidst a joyous reunion, Irene relates to her father all her adventures, letting him understand what a vital role Curdie had played in them. As Curdie then warns them of the impending flood that the goblins have devised, the party narrowly escapes up the mountainside as the onrushing waters, entering their home through the tunnel the goblins had dug, destroys it. The king offers to reward Curdie by making him a part of his bodyguard, but it is determined that staying at home and serving his parents is his rightful place. Many of the goblins were drowned in the flood; the few that survive grow milder in mind and heart, becoming "very much like the Scotch Brownies."

What is there, then, about this tale that made a difference to Chesterton's "whole existence," as he affirmed? Its themes are, of course, very basic to a Christian view of life, and they are winsomely and compellingly expressed. They include the importance of a personal relationship and trust in God, his caring concern for one's well-being, a sensitivity to his leading, and the importance of unquestioning obedience. But it is to be doubted that these are what Chesterton had primarily in mind.

The strength and abiding value of the tale lies in the nature of its tone, its almost mesmerizing simplicity and purity. This chaste atmosphere is most strongly present in those scenes of Irene visiting her aged fairy grandmother. To read them is to feel as though one is breathing oxygenized air.

This is the quality of true myth. It is as though one has caught a glimpse of Ultimate Reality. To quote Chesterton, it is "the most real, the most realistic, in the exact sense of the phrase the most like life," that is, life at its very heart, rightly experienced.

4

The Princess and Curdie

Christ is our righteousness, not that we should escape punishment, still less escape being righteous, but as the live potent creator of righteousness in us, so that we, with our wills receiving his spirit, shall like him resist unto blood, striving against sin; shall know in ourselves, as he knows, what a lovely thing is righteousness, what a mean, ugly unnatural thing is unrighteousness. He is our righteousness, and that righteousness is no fiction, no pretense, no imputation. "The Last Farthing," *Unspoken Sermons: Second Series.*

The White Pigeon: Chapters 1–2

The final sentence of *The Princess and the Goblin* promises that more of the story of Curdie will be forthcoming, and *The Princess and Curdie* appears ten years later, in 1882. In it MacDonald gives definitive expression to one of his favorite themes: the nature of true Christian heroism, i.e., the life that in scriptural terms overcomes. Foundational to it is childlike faith. He remarks early on: "The child is not meant to die, but to be forever fresh-born."

The initial chapter focuses the reader's imagination upon the dual character of mountains, bringing into sharp contrast their beautiful exteriors with the dark and mysterious energies within. Whereas in the prior tale they seemed at the beginning to be metaphors for the human psyche, here they seem to suggest mankind conceived in terms of their spiritual potentialities; they are "beautiful terrors," with lovely surfaces hiding inner caldrons filled with energies of great possibilities, both for good and bad. Individuals are like miners who explore their depths and bring forth that which they can use either for good or evil. One is alerted to look in the story not only for how in human experience the outer world belies the inner—how appearances belie reality—but also for the being/becoming theme: how forbidding energies may be transformed either into that which is both useful and beautiful, or that which is otherwise. A person's orientation to spiritual reality determines the difference.

Curdie needs the proper orientation. In the second chapter we are re-minded how in the prior tale he had been unable to see the Princess Irene's great-great-grandmother. As a consequence, the older he grew the more he doubted. Believing less and less in that which he could not see, "he was gradually changing into a commonplace man."

With increasing pride in his own resources, one evening out with his bow and arrow he shoots a beautiful white pigeon. The seemingly off-hand event initiates a momentous change in him, for he is struck, as he gazes upon the fading eyes of the bird, with powerful feelings of guilt. What has he really done? MacDonald writes: "underground waters gushed from the boy's heart," and the reader recalls the initial mountain imagery. Momen-tarily he summons his inner bravado, but then "a great globe of light" ap-pears in the evening sky. Recalling how he saw it before when he was with Irene, he runs full speed towards the castle in which Irene had met that mysterious ancient woman.

"What Am I to Call You?": Chapters 3–4

After climbing stair after stair, Curdie finally reaches the very top of the tower. Being all but mesmerized as he hears behind a certain door the en-chanting sound of a spinning wheel, he knocks and is admitted into a room flooded with moonlight, suggesting the enrapturing glory of the divine presence.

The crooked and withered form of the aged lady that Curdie encoun-ters, however, at first strikes him as far from glorious, but when he sees her eyes, "all the laugh went out of him." A person's perception of the nature of God changes when one gives it close and earnest attention. She begins to question him, eliciting his confession as he holds out to her the dead bird. The scene contains a wealth of theological truths, vividly underscored by its emotional intensity: confession must be complete and heartfelt; people who act without any intention to be better are "doing everything wrong"; evil acts have such a character that good can come out of them;[1] confession and restitution bring great relief and joy; grateful obedience is to follow forgiveness; and grace is effective in and through a life to the extent that it meets with full submission to the divine will ("I will see what I can do for you—only the *canning* depends on yourself").

Curdie is astonished to see the old lady now stand before him as a resplendent lady, full of grace and beauty. Every trace of her former withered and decrepit appearance has disappeared. People see according to their natures, and one's perception of the nature of God is quite dependent upon one's attitude and relationship to him.[2] She then tests his willingness to obey her by giving him something not to do: never to laugh or make fun of her, but to "hold his tongue" if he should hear anyone speak denigratingly of her. Puzzled, Curdie asks, "What am I to call you?" only to have her disappear from his sight. Gripped suddenly with a great fear, he finds his way in the dark down from the tower and safely to his home. Such encounters with the divine presence are matters of faith, and must rest on faith alone, rather than on intellectual analysis.

Curdie's Struggle to Obey: Chapters 5–7

After Curdie tells his parents his adventure and questions whether it all has been a dream, they encourage him to obey the old lady's behest. Such occasion soon occurs, as Curdie and his father are present with a large group of miners who tell many dark tales of one they call "Old Mother Wotherwop." Curdie successfully refrains from joining in their gossiping and resists their jeering at him when he does so. The miners perceive her nature according to theirs.

Momentarily remaining behind as the miners leave the mine, Curdie and his father are privileged to be confronted with an "Emerald Lady," an exceedingly beautiful face appearing in a cloud of golden green and emitting a glorious aura of rainbow colors. Curdie knows by her eyes that she is Irene's great-great-grandmother, and he feels that "all the beauty of the

1. Cf. Rom 5:19–6:2.
2. Cf. Ps 18:25–26.

cavern, yes, of all he knew of the whole creation, seemed gathered in one center of harmony and loveliness in the person of the ancient lady who stood before him in the very summer of beauty and strength."

When he wants to know where the light comes from, she disappears, and Curdie and his father are shrouded in deep darkness. They grow anxious as they wait for an extended period of time, until a faint green light appears in the distance, gradually grows more splendid, and the cavern is again blazing with lights. Again, the text suggests that intellectual inquisitions are not helpful.

As they enter into conversation, she tells them that they have royal blood in their veins, and that Curdie is being trained for an important task. When Curdie tells her of his confusion as to who she really is, as she seems to have so many identities, she explains that, since people perceive her according to their natures, all the appearances she uses are inadequate. He asks then if she would give him some sign whereby he would always recognize her, but she refuses, explaining: "that would be to keep you from knowing me," as the sign would inevitably be substituted in his mind for her person. She explains: "You must do what you can to know me, and if you do, you will. You shall see me again—in very different circumstances from these, and, I will tell you so much, it *may* be in a very different shape." She then disappears, leading them by means of a green star safely out of the mountain. As they proceed, they meet an old countrywoman whom Curdie recognizes as but another appearance, and she bids him come to her in the dove tower the following night. The existential dimensions of one's relations with God could hardly be better symbolized.

Roses That Burn: Chapter 8

The symbolic richness of the scene that follows renders it one of the very finest MacDonald ever penned, fraught as it is with penetrating insights into the intimate dimensions of an individual disciple's relationship to and fellowship with God. Curdie obeys the old lady's summons, and after some difficulties getting by the housekeeper, finds his way into her chambers. Obeying a voice that bids him enter, he opens the door and is astonished to find no room there—no walls or even a floor—but when the voice repeats the summons, he steps straight in, and "that which had need of the floor found it, and his foot was satisfied." Obedience to God's behests demands complete faith in his provisions; it discovers its needs to be supplied only after it ventures forth.

Within, he sees at first, not the grandmother, but her beautiful spinning wheel, an image suggesting the providence of God. She asks him what the wheel is saying, and when he concentrates his attention, he hears the lady's voice singing a beautiful song, the gist of which is an assuring affirmation that all aspects and events in nature and in people's lives are working harmoniously, not only toward the great "day when the sleepers shall rise," but also towards a glorious but ineffable reality, "the something that nobody knows!"

Next, Curdie is subjected to a severe and painful trial. On the hearth "a great fire was burning, and the fire was a huge heap of roses, and yet it was fire." He is told to thrust his hands into it. She warns it will hurt him terribly, but "much good" will come to him from it. The act being "too terrible to think about," he rushes to obey, and the effect is all but overwhelming pain, but when it becomes so severe he feels he can no longer endure it, it subsides. His hands are now "white and smooth like the princess's." Looking at the grandmother, he sees she has been weeping, and in answer to his query she reveals she has felt the same pain he did.[3] Those whom God calls and ordains for a certain mission must be refined for the task; painful experience may be required, but God shares the pain.

Curdie is given hands that enable him to discern the spiritual state of any individual with whom his mission will require him to interact. She explains to him that all people, "if they do not take care," are going downhill to "the animal's country." The imagery expresses a concept at the heart of MacDonald's theology. All people are on a spiritual continuum, as it were, either getting better or worse; their acts—which their hands (i.e., what they *do*) signify—determine their spiritual states. But she warns not to be hasty in judging which direction any given individual is going, as "two people may be at the same spot in manners and behavior, and yet one may be getting better and the other worse."

Curdie is given solemn warnings as to how he is to use the gift he has been given. If he should ever use it simply for "his own ends," it will be taken from him and, not realizing that is the case, will be "in a far worse condition than before." And—with few exceptions—he is not expected to warn those whom he discerns are retrogressing. When Curdie asks why a person should not be warned, the grandmother summons Lina—a grotesque being

3. Cf. Isa 63:9: "In all their affliction he was afflicted . . ."

composed of various distorted animal parts, "ludicrous" in her "horrible mass of incongruities." Grasping its paw, he is amazed that it felt like the "neat little hand of a child!" The old lady refuses to answer more of Curdie's questions, except to remark: "The paw in your hand now might almost teach you the whole science of natural history—the heavenly sort, I mean."

The incident depicts MacDonald's hope that all people, no matter how morally distorted creatures they may become, do not lose the capacity to turn and begin the long, slow process of rising from the "animal's country" they had descended in to. Lina, who will figure in Curdie's mission, is a fascinating depiction of this theological conjecture. Out of the sinful depths that shaped her deformities she has turned and begun to ascend; the help she will offer to Curdie will demonstrate her change of attitude. It will "pull the child out of the beast."

The great-great-grandmother gives Curdie instructions as to how his father may be called upon to help him and then tells him that on the morrow he must set out for the king's court. In response to his request for more specific instructions as to the nature of his mission, she rather sternly tells him he has orders enough, that as he goes along he will find what he needs to do. He has one idea of his work; she has another, and he must allow her idea to set his right as he proceeds. The scene again emphasizes the existential dimensions to Christian discipleship.

Curdie's Discoveries: Chapters 9–22

The following morning, with the blessing of his parents, Curdie sets out on his mission. Soon Lina joins him and proves to be a great companion as she saves him from several threatening disasters. Along the way they are joined by a host of grotesque creatures not unlike Lina. When they arrive in Gwyntystorm, they find a city neglected, with the people given over to materialism and greed. Curdie's encounters with an inhospitable baker, a barber, and a butcher with his dogs, show how self-centered, belligerent, and rude the people tend to be. He and Lina, however, are kindly received for a night by an hospitable old woman, Derba, and Barbara, her grandchild.

The next morning a crowd assembles at the door and a magistrate reads a summons that Curdie is to be tried and his animal roasted alive. In the turmoil that follows, Lina frightens the crowd away and disappears, but Curdie is arrested and locked up. When a crowd again assembles, Lina suddenly appears, scattering them. Curdie then tunnels away with his mattock until they are able to escape, finding themselves in the wine cellar of the king's palace.

Cautiously moving through the servant's quarters, they find nothing but sloth, filth, and disorder. Rising stealthily, they come into the king's bedroom, where Curdie encounters Irene, who happily greets him. He discovers that she is keeping watch over the old king her father, who is sick, feeble, and fearful lest he be overthrown. Curdie discovers that the doctor who attends the king is secretly poisoning him, and he contrives a scheme whereby he can secure healthy food for his highness.

Braving the dangers of the city streets, Curdie retrieves a loaf of bread from the bakery and manages to convey it back to the king, who partakes of it and revives sufficiently to refuse the Lord Chamberlain's attempt to persuade him to sign a document that would have relinquished his powers. Meanwhile, on an errand to secure some more wholesome food, Curdie discovers that the tunnels under the castle rocks contain fragments of gold. He calculates that now he has access to the resource that, properly mined, would allow the king to rid himself of the horde of dishonest and scheming servants in his employ.

The Vengeance: Chapters 23–28

Curdie now undertakes the huge task of setting things right. He meets a servant girl whom he discovers wants to be true and do right, and he commissions her to warn the staff that they must turn from their evil ways, which she duly does. He then foils an attempt on the part of Dr. Kelman to further poison the king. Meanwhile, Lina summons a host of grotesque creatures similar to herself, termed the Avengers, who under Curdie's direction, set about soundly trouncing the evil servants and driving them from the palace and cleansing it.

The various depictions of how the grotesque creatures wreak vengeance upon the courtiers who have devised an elaborate plot to usurp power from the king are fine instances of MacDonald's imaginative verve. In a series of fantastic scenes the authorities are all expelled. As they were unable to find shelter in the village for the night, Derba, the old woman who had befriended Curdie earlier when he first came into Gwyntystorm, opens her doors to them. As a reward for her hospitality, Curdie requests her to go to the palace and become the king's chatelaine, the mistress of the castle.

MacDonald now seizes an opportunity to hold up to ridicule what he saw to be the gist of the established church of his day. In the chapter entitled "The Preacher" he depicts a clergyman preaching on the text, "Honesty is the best policy," maintaining that all society would be in a blissful state if that simple principle were observed. At the height of his eloquence a "leg-serpent," snatches him by his vestments and drops him into a dust hole, where he becomes a lunatic. Next, a conclave of priests decide a great exorcism is needed to rid the palace staff of the demons that have possessed them; then the monarchy should be replaced by a group of governors who would rule justly. But in the night before they could execute their plan, some of the horde of grotesque beings effect fantastic justice upon many of the miscreants of Gwyntystorm.

The Restoration: Chapters 29–34

Meanwhile the king is gradually regaining his health, greatly helped by the child Barbara, whose companionship he finds therapeutic. The lord chancellor, however, flees to the neighboring kingdom to enlist the help of its army in his scheme to depose the king. Back at the mountain cottage, Peter is summoned—as the great-great-grandmother had told him he might be—to come to his son's aid.

One night Curdie is awakened by a dull red radiance and, thinking the king's chamber may be on fire, enters to be confronted by a conflagration of "glowing, flaming roses, red and white," with the king lying motionless but sobbing in its midst. Above him hovers the faint form of the old princess, weeping, while her tears quietly douse the flames. She then gently lifts the king and returns him to his bed. Curdie, filled with joy at what he has seen, sinks into a dreamless sleep.

Completely refreshed, the king dons his armor and prepares for battle. He and his small company proceed, including the Princess Irene upon her white pony and Curdie, followed by his company of Uglies. A fierce battle follows, as the king's group is aided by the sudden appearance of a great flock of white pigeons, apparently commanded by the princess waving her arms. When the princess is in danger, Peter suddenly appears to defend her, and victory is secured.

There are shades of MacDonald's eschatology in the scene that follows, as the king has the company of evil men set before him and addresses them: "Ye slaves. . . . I would have freed you, but ye would not be free. Now shall ye be ruled with a rod of iron, that ye may learn what freedom is, and love it and seek it." Those who have failed in this life to use their free will rightly will in the next be trained under more rigorous circumstances.[4]

A Startling Conclusion: Chapter 35

The king establishes a righteous rule, financed by mining the gold Curdie had discovered under the palace. He commissions Curdie as his heir apparent, with the expressed desire that he and Irene will one day wed. As the company sits down to supper, a housemaid serves them wine. When she looks Curdie in the eyes, he in joy recognizes her as another appearance of the great-great-grandmother who has been their guiding and protecting force. As the company all kneel in homage, she bids them sit down and proceeds to serve them all.

Now termed Queen Irene, she is seldom absent from the palace, ready to help anyone who seeks her, but spending part of her time "with the dear old Uglies in the wood. . . . and with others there as well." On the basis of MacDonald's theology, one can infer that they represent souls who "have gone downhill to the animal's country" and are, under her surveillance, learning to choose righteously. The purpose of the afterlife is not punishment for punishment's sake, but rather for the sake of learning to choose the good and obeying righteous causes.

As Curdie one day seeks her, he finds her and Lina in the uppermost room of the palace beside a glorious fire filled with red and white roses. At the right moment Lina casts herself in it and is seen no more as Lina. Apparently, having demonstrated her obedience in the cause of right as she has, she has come to the moment of final purging and transformation. As the mysterious fire had earlier purified Curdie, so now it cleanses her.

In time the old king dies, and Curdie and Irene are married and rule righteously. However, they have no children, and then a king arises whose only interest is the acquisition of more and more gold. His greed depletes the mine under the city, and it eventually falls into the cavity to its total destruction. The "very name of Gwyntystorm" ceases "from the lips of men."

The abrupt conclusion, which goes counter to the happy ending convention of fairy tales, may strike a reader as puzzling. Both it and the disappearance of Lina need to be understood in terms of the entire gist of MacDonald's theology. With Gwyntystorm's demise he is making a

4. Cf. e.g., Rev 2:26–27.

powerful statement concerning human responsibility in regards to the nature and enduring threat of evil. Constant vigilance, together with a steady pursuance of the good, must never be relaxed.

5

The Wise Woman,
or A Double Story

. . . we must refuse, abandon, deny self altogether as a ruling, or
determining, or originating element in us. It is no longer the regent
of our action. . . . It must not be its own law; Christ must be its law.
The time will come when it shall be so possessed, so enlarged, so
idealized, by the indwelling God, who is its deeper, its deepest self,
that there will be no longer any enforced denial of it needful. "Self-
Denial," *Unspoken Sermons: Series II*

In George MacDonald's theology, the essence of salvation is the complete transformation of the self. The self must be freed from its illusions of independence and self-sufficiency and be completely remade into a righteous being. In other words, the self must be born again. This transformation is a long and difficult process, one that should be begun in this life, but will not be completed until the afterlife, a subject MacDonald explores more fully in *Lilith*.

In "The Wise Woman" he is showing how difficult and demanding the process is. Published in 1876, its original title was "A Double Story," being a tale of two girls, the one the daughter of a shepherd and his wife who was raised in humble surroundings, the other the daughter of a king and queen, raised in the opulence of the palace. Both are pampered by their parents to see themselves as "Somebody." The blame for this damning illusion is placed solidly upon each set of parents who fostered the deception in their children and exercised no discipline or restraining influence to move them away from their overarching egotism.

A mysterious woman abducts each and exposes them to a series of experiences that work to disillusion them and gradually begin the transforming process that enables each to become spiritually healthy, altruistic beings. She is not an allegorical figure, but, similar to the aged woman in the Curdie stories, she suggests simply the Divine Presence working providentially in human experience, in which people constantly face situations and circumstances to which they must respond. Those who react selfishly, concerned only with their self-advantage, strengthen the hold the damning illusion of egotism has upon them; those who respond altruistically and with self-abandon, having the welfare of fellow beings in mind, are taking steps towards the final goal of spiritual maturity.

To each set of parents the Wise Woman issues a stern rebuke: they have treated their children badly—all their supposedly loving intentions notwithstanding. Rosamond, the princess who grows up amidst the opulence of the palace, quickly becomes covetous and greedy, then gluttonous, bored, and filled with ennui; Agnes, the shepherd's child who grows up in a rural setting amidst modest means and plays with a few simple toys, is free from avariciousness, gluttony, and boredom, but she, nevertheless, is immoderately conceited due to the parents' doting upon her.

Only Severity Will Save Her

The first part of the tale presents the Wise Woman's patient efforts to release Rosamond from her imprisonment to her self. She at first tries kindness, but the princess does "not in the least understand" it. In a further attempt to liberate her from "her own miserable Somebody," the Wise Woman sings her a song of the sufferings of a forlorn moon, but Rosamond responds with hatred. She is convinced that the wise woman is an ogress, intent on eating her.

MacDonald is reminding his readers that such a being as Rosamond is not at all inclined to understand kindness and sees only base motives in altruistic acts. A person in which evil thoughts predominate is confined to seeing all things as evil. After he has depicted Rosamond in her spiritual blindness as violently kicking and screaming, he boldly remarks, "as those of my readers who are of the same sort as herself will consider the right and natural thing to do." MacDonald is determined to drive the point home to his audience.

The tale stresses that the process of effecting any spiritual change in a person's character is exceedingly slow, and any changes effected are insubstantial. With indefatigable patience and persistence the Wise Woman places Rosamond in situations of aloneness and deprivation, instructing her that some simple act such as knocking on a door would give her access to shelter and food. But the princess stubbornly resists until, finally overcome with hunger and fear, she submits. However, no sooner than she is received into the Wise Woman's arms and gains release, she regresses to her old attitudes of rebellion and scorn.

Each succeeding situation in which the Wise Woman places Rosamond is more rigorous and demanding than the former, and in each a little moral progress is achieved, followed by a retrogression. As she begins faintly to feel some love for her parents and some degree of trust in the kind intentions of the Wise Woman, it occurs to her that she has grown to become a very good person, and her self-admiration not only prevents further progress but also increases her suspicions that the Wise Woman is only wanting to fatten and eat her.

More situations follow, in which the Wise Woman leaves Rosamond alone, gives her explicit instructions with the condition she will not be able to eat until she completely obeys. Each is more rigorous than the former. The cycle of reluctant obedience and subsequent satisfaction continues; after each Rosamond returns to her recalcitrant and suspicious attitudes. But little by little some slight spiritual milestone is passed. On one occasion she discovers a picture of a girl playing in an idyllic rural scene and wishes that she were that girl. Suddenly, she finds the wish come true.

A Worse Case

The narrator then turns our attention to Agnes. The two girls are alike in their overweening narcissism but, whereas Rosamond is subject to a variety of moods, Agnes is steadfast in her "calm assured self-satisfaction." By giving us two girls who exist in antithetical social and economic environments but are possessed of the same self-assuredness, MacDonald is emphasizing that the affliction is universal.

Agnes comes to understand her condition much more quickly than did Rosamond, but her affliction is yet more severe. When the Wise Woman places beside Agnes a very ugly child that mimics her, she hates it, then is aware that the child is "her Self, her Somebody," and is filled with shame. But the Wise Woman warns her that just because she feels shame she is not cured, and assigns her a task. When she performs it, she again thinks herself "Somebody." Then, seeing a picture of a great city and a marble palace, she intensely wishes she were there, thinking how generous she would be in those circumstances. The narrator comments that Agnes was now worse than Rosamond ever had been, because she retrogressed from her prior shame into an attitude that "was as bad as ever, therefore worse than before." Spiritual lapses are serious affairs. With patient persistence, the Wise Woman grants her wish, and Agnes finds herself in the great city.

Possessed with her seemingly incurable conceit, Agnes is given a place among the palace servants. Learning that the king and queen were searching for their princess and coming to suspect she must be staying with her father and mother, she tries to tell the king and queen and is not believed. But the king commands that the shepherd and his wife be brought to the palace.

The two girls now are each in the former home of the other. Rosamond gradually progresses in her new-found rural environment. Her romping in the open air with a shepherd dog—an incarnation of the Wise Woman— that "shepherds" her is spiritually salutary. Communion with nature also changes her noticeably. But when Prince the dog disappears, the shepherdess loses patience with her and commands her to be gone. Endeavoring to find her way back to the palace, she encounters more trials. Each is shaped by the skillful and patient guidance of the Wise Woman, and through repeated moral lapses Rosamond is brought to the end of herself.

When Rosamond turns to the Wise Woman and asks for help, determined now to become a better person, a great milestone is passed. Then, gradually responding more commendably to future trials, she comes to realize that the Wise Woman has been present in various disguises in all her ordeals. Feeling shame for her past, she asks the Wise Woman for forgiveness, and asks: "How could you love such an ugly, ill-tempered, rude, hateful little wretch?" "'I saw, through it all, what you were going to be,' said the wise woman, kissing her. 'But remember you have yet only *begun* to be what I saw.'"

Now that all the parties are together in the palace, the tale is brought to its conclusion. Agnes and her parents are reunited, but, when the king learns that Rosamond has been with the shepherd and shepherdess and they have tried to teach her some duties, he condemns them to death. Rosamond intercedes for them, and the king and queen recognize her as their own.

Then the Wise Woman appears and solidly condemns both sets of parents for their failures to properly teach their children. The shepherd dies; Agnes, who has much yet to learn, is sent home with her mother; and Rosamond is charged to serve her parents for their moral improvement.

In case the reader muses that this "double story" is considerably more directly didactic than traditional fairy tales are, MacDonald gives his purpose at the conclusion. The narrator remarks that he has already "told more than is good for those who read but with their foreheads, and enough for those whom it has made look a little solemn, and sigh as they close the book." He is determined to emphasize the crucial importance of the fantasy's central theme.

In his novel *Malcolm*, which was published in 1875, the year prior to the appearance of "A Double Story," MacDonald accosts the "worshipper of Art" who objects to his voice directly addressing the reader in his narratives as being "an offence to utter in the temple of Art." MacDonald replies:

> Not against Art, I think: but if it be an offence to the worshipper of Art, let him keep silence before his goddess; for me, I am a sweeper of the floors in the temple of Life, and his goddess is my mare, and shall go in the dust-cart.[1]

He is determined that his art serve Life (capitalized). This story is a fine example of art performing that office as it incorporates the author's voice in the narrative.

1. Chapter 38.

6

At the Back of the North Wind

We have no reason to distrust our world, for it is not against us. If it has terrors, they are our terrors. If it has an abyss, it is ours. If dangers are there, we must try to love them. And if we would live with faith in the value of what is challenging, then what now appears to us as most alien will become our truest, most trustworthy friend. Let us not forget the ancient myths at the outset of humanity's journey, the myths about dragons that at the last moment transform into princesses. Perhaps all the dragons of our lives are princesses who are only waiting to see us act just once with beauty and courage. Perhaps every terror is, in its deepest essence, something that needs our recognition or help. —Rainer Maria Rilke, *Letters to a Young Poet*[1]

The Hayloft: Chapter 1

At the Back of the North Wind, which began to be serialized in 1868 and was published in book form in 1871, was written during a period when MacDonald was giving concentrated attention to the problem of how the adversities and sufferings of life could be justified in terms of the love of God.[2] The tale arises out of his personal experience and is his definitive statement on this issue. A man of weak constitution who suffered

---

1. Rilke, *Letters to a Young Poet*, 69.

2. The novels *The Seaboard Parish* and *Guild Court*, written shortly before, also explore the problem of suffering.

several ailments, he fell seriously ill during a yachting trip in 1869, had to be abruptly returned, and had an extended period of convalescence. Thus this fantasy has an especially strong autobiographical aspect.

For a fantasy to have a satisfying aesthetic effect, the author must carefully create at the very beginning an atmosphere that entices the reader with the reality of the other world, making it both believable and inviting. MacDonald does so immediately in his opening paragraph, in which the narrator announces that his purpose is to describe a boy's experience who actually went to the back of the north wind. He disrobes this image of its novelty by referring to an "old Greek writer" who described that region. The writer is Herodotus, "the father of history" who in the fifth century BC told about the hyperboreans, an ancient people inhabiting the far north, beyond the home of the north wind. They lived idyllic lives there in complete happiness. In fact, their happiness was so intense that, according to Herodotus, they drowned themselves.

Our narrator surmises that Herodotus must have given an incorrect account, for we now have a differing version upon the authority of a boy who actually went there. The reader's interest is immediately piqued concerning the nature of this higher, remote realm. MacDonald has introduced facts that are both believable and curious, so that we find ourselves being imaginatively open to new truths and desirous of receiving them.

Diamond lives contentedly amid conditions of appalling poverty. Because his father is a coachman who houses his family in a meager coach house, Diamond's bed is in a hay mow in the loft, above the horse stall. The thin boards of the walls have cracks between them and knot holes through which the wind flows freely. But Diamond snuggles in the warmth of his bed, listens to the great horse—also named Diamond—munching his hay below, and thinks "what a happy boy he was." That Diamond the boy shares the same name with the horse below him is another fact that is both curious and believable. Its significance will appear later.

One evening Diamond thinks he hears a voice calling to him, engages it in conversation, and finds himself in the presence of a woman both forbidding and very beautiful:

> He stood up in terror. Leaning over him was the large beautiful
> pale face of a woman. Her dark eyes looked a little angry, for they
> had just begun to flash; but a quivering in her sweet upper lip
> made her look as if she were going to cry. What was most strange
> was that away from her head streamed out her black hair in every

direction, so that the darkness in the hay-loft looked as if it were made of her hair; but as Diamond gazed at her in speechless amazement, mingled with confidence—for the boy was entranced with her mighty beauty—her hair began to gather itself out of the darkness, and fell down all about her again, till her face looked out of the midst of it like a moon out of a cloud. From her eyes came all the light by which Diamond saw her face and her hair.

MacDonald is at his best in such descriptions, creating as they do an atmosphere at once of awe, intrigue, and desire. The impact is mythic. That the north wind is an archetypal image for divinely ordained adversity is, of course, something a child does not know. The imagery describing this initial encounter creates a set of positive attitudes towards her. "Nobody is cold with the North Wind," she assures him. Most people "are cold because they are not with the North Wind, but without it."

She invites him into an intimate relationship of adventure and utter trust. That he must first give her his name suggests that he must see himself rightly and understand his own significance. A diamond is not only a precious object of appreciable value, but its value is related to its biblical significance: in the Old Testament a diamond has a prominent place on the high priest's breastplate. The subtle reference to Scripture signals that the symbolic significance of images to come may well be discovered by having a knowledge of their import in the Bible.

The themes of this fantasy are shaped by the biblical admonitions concerning the trials and adversities of life. MacDonald's original inspiration must have come from the book of Job: "You lift me up on the wind, you make me ride on it, and you toss me about in the roar of the storm. I know that you will bring me to death, and to the house appointed for all living."[3] The New Testament counsels positive attitudes—even joyous ones—towards trials. We read in the Letter of James: "My brothers and sisters, whenever you face trials of any kind, consider it nothing but joy, because you know that the testing of your faith produces endurance; and let endurance have its full effect, so that you may be mature and complete, lacking in nothing"; and Paul writes in his Letter to the Romans: ". . . we boast in our hope of sharing the glory of God. And not only that, but we also boast in our sufferings, knowing that suffering produces endurance, and endurance produces character, and character produces hope, and hope

---

3. Job 30:22–23.

does not disappoint us, because God's love has been poured into our hearts
. . ."[4] Peter's epistles have similar admonitions. To instill such attitudes
within the heart of a child requires considerable skill, and this fantasy rises
to the occasion.

In her initial meeting with Diamond, North Wind seeks to create
some very basic attitudes. Foundational to them all is a canny awareness
that the outer appearances of things seldom coincide with their underlying
reality: appearances are often deceptive. MacDonald introduces this fact to
him very early in the text when the narrator remarks: ". . . to know a person's name is not always to know the person's self," and the admonition is
implicit in much of the imagery of the fantasy. Diamond must not be eager
to go with her simply because she is beautiful—for beautiful things may
be untrustworthy. He must be assured that she is good as well as beautiful.

The converse is true as well: that which appears ugly can be beautiful
at heart. Although she may appear ugly to him, he must nevertheless trust
her completely: ". . . if I change into a serpent or a tiger, you must not let
go your hold of me, for my hand will never change in yours if you keep a
good hold. If you keep a hold, you will know who I am all the time, even
when you look at me and can't see me the least like the North Wind. I may
look something very awful." For most people, she has to be ugly in order
that the good she intends be effective. Complete trust in her goodness in all
circumstances is utterly essential. He is repeatedly told never to let go of her
hand. When Diamond says he understands, she bids him come with her.

"I Had to Make Myself Look Like a Bad Thing": Chapters 2–4

Diamond's first attempt to go with North Wind, however, ends in his dismay. Going from the loft out onto the yard, he looks for her in vain. Beginning to cry in his loneliness, he is rescued by the nurse who works for the
neighbors, the Colemans, and is restored to his bed. When he awakes the
following morning he is uncertain as to whether or not his recollections of
North Wind were not simply a dream.

A second dismay follows. Going down the ladder in the morning into
the stable below, he scampers onto the back of sleeping Diamond the horse.
Frightened, the horse rears up and Diamond in terror clings to his mane
until the horse settles and he is rescued by his loving mother. These initial

---

4. Jas 1:2–4; Rom 5:2b–5.

frustrations are necessary for him to come into more mature understanding of life. He later learns that North Wind was present in the gentle breeze behind the primroses, and that he must learn how to respect the horse's nature in order to control it properly.

Diamond the boy is most at home when he is properly situated on the back of both the horse and North Wind; that is, when he learns to be rightly related to their true natures. As the story progresses, he learns both how to cooperate with and affirm the activities of North Wind, and also how to care for the horse and appropriate its energies to his own purposes. It is only after he has mastered these lessons that he can and does become a strong influence for good in the lives of his parents and of all whom he meets. The fantasy is a type of *Bildungsroman*—a story that traces how the central character grows into assuming a mature and productive role in life—of which there are many in nineteenth-century fiction. Charles Dickens's *David Copperfield* is a prime example.

The North Wind and Diamond the horse are symbols that encompass a great deal of life. North Wind suggests life's adversities: all the seemingly negative occurrences—both large and small—that simply happen, beyond one's conscious control. Diamond the horse, on the other hand, suggests the natural world—that part of life which does fall under one's control, over which a person must learn to be a good steward. The identity of names suggests how much a part of the natural world Diamond the boy is.

For Diamond to be rightly related to the natural world, he must have an intimate and comfortable relation with the supernatural. When on her second coming to him North Wind states she must embark on a more difficult mission, she makes a nest for him in her long, luxurious hair. The image of his snuggling into it suggests the comfort and sense of protection that children long to feel.

Such a close and trusting relation to her is essential for him to be prepared for, and not to be dismayed at, the various guises which she must assume. On this second visit she first comes to him not as a full-grown woman but as a young girl. Her first task, as they glide through a hall of a large home, is to appear as a frightening wolf to a nurse who is abusing a child in her care. When Diamond voices his dismay, North Wind explains that such startling appearance was necessary for the accomplishing of her task: "I had to make myself look like a bad thing before she could see me. . . . Good people see good things; bad people bad things."[5] The various masks

---

5. Chapter 3.

through which grace appears are determined by the nature of the person to whom it comes. The psalmist David presents the principle: "With the loyal you show yourself loyal; with the blameless you show yourself blameless; with the pure you show yours self pure; and with the crooked you show yourself perverse."[6]

When Diamond wonders why she is kinder to him than to the nurse, she responds, "Everybody can't be done to all the same. Everybody is not ready for the same thing." That Diamond is a good-hearted child is shown by his reactions to the little street-sweeper girl that they espy being blown about by the blustery wind. As soon as he sees her he wants to help her and is willing to leave North Wind to do so. We learn later in the text that the girl's name is Nanny. She, like Diamond, is victim to a poverty-stricken life, but one appreciably more pitiful. She stands in contrast to him in that, when he tells her of his adventures with North Wind, she thinks him crazy and refuses his urging to become acquainted with her. As a consequence, Nanny's adversities become yet more intense, as her experiences later in the plot will reveal.

North Wind Sinks a Ship: Chapters 5–8

In chapter 5, Diamond's father places him on the back of Diamond the horse. He feels "a little tremulous" at first, but he soon learns that "as he was obedient to his father, so the horse was obedient to him," and is pleased to learn how he can control the horse. He is acquiring proper attitudes towards the natural world as well as the supernatural.

Diamond learns next that adversities come in a great range of intensities. He is in the neighbor's summer garden when North Wind appears to him so small and unassuming he mistakes her for a fairy who is caring for a bee. To his dismay, however, she informs him her task that night is to sink a ship, and although he expresses his hope that he does not have to go with her, she tells him he must. When he longs to be assured that she cannot be cruel, she responds: "No; I could not be cruel if I would. I can do nothing cruel, although I often do what looks like cruel to those who do not know what I really am doing. The people they say I drown, I only carry away to–to–to–well, the back of the North Wind. . . ," a place she says she has never seen and knows nothing about, although she knows the way.[7]

---

6. Ps 18:25–26.

7. Chapter 5. MacDonald is here restating the principle announced in the final

In her being a servant figure who simply carries out her orders but has very limited knowledge about their import, she differs from the great-great-grandmother of the Curdie stories. The ancient grandmother is quite clearly an image of the sacramental presence of God in life; North Wind is simply an angelic servant. When she says that she has heard a rumor "it is all managed by a baby," MacDonald is echoing his image of God as a child arranging balls in "The Golden Key."

When in chapter 6 North Wind comes that night and takes him with her into an intense storm, Diamond's consternation returns, and he persists in voicing his dismay that sinking a ship is not like the North Wind he has come to know. It is simply unlike the being he has come to know and trust. She reasons with him that since the being he knows is good, and since it is impossible that there be "two mes," the "other me you don't know must be as kind as the me you do know." Diamond's submissive response is theologically nuanced: "I love you, and you must love me, or else why would I have started loving you? How could you know how to put on such a beautiful face if you did not love me and the rest? You may sink as many ships as you like." Although the lightning blinds and the thunder deafens him as they fly on through the storm, he laughs and is content, for she is holding him to her bosom.

North Wind further consoles him at the beginning of chapter 7 when she envisions the outcome: "I am always hearing, through every noise, through all the noise I'm making myself even, the sound of a far off song. I do not exactly know where it is, or what it means . . . but what I do hear, is quite enough to make me able to bear the cry from the drowning ship. So it would you if you could hear it."

MacDonald is indeed undertaking a difficult subject, but if he is to succeed in fully establishing in a child's mind a biblical attitude towards all adversity, suffering, and death itself, he has little choice. For biblical confirmation of his theological position, MacDonald would no doubt refer to such passages as: "I am the Lord, and there is no other. I form light and create darkness, I make weal and create woe; I the Lord do all these things," and: "Does disaster befall a city, unless the Lord has done it?" The "far off song" that consoles North Wind herself is suggested in the Revelation to St. John, when after the judgments upon earth have all been executed, the hosts of heaven sing: "Great and amazing are you deeds, Lord God the Almighty!

---

sentence of *Phantastes*:"What we call evil, is the only and best shape, which, for the person and his condition at the time, could be assumed by the best good."

Just and true are your ways, King of the nations! Lord, who will not fear and glorify your name? For you alone are holy. All nations will come and worship before you, for your judgments have been revealed." A person can hardly expect that MacDonald would erect a complete theological treatise in a fairy tale, but this story is impressively crafted.[8]

To avoid Diamond's witnessing the sinking of the ship, North Wind deposits him in a cathedral while she executes her mission. When he finds himself on a narrow ledge high up in the dome and cannot feel North Wind's presence, he panics; then he is suddenly aware that he is in North Wind's arms. Questioned as to why she left him, she replies, "Because I wanted you to walk alone." The Christian is not fortified with the consciousness of strength given before the event, to be stored up, as it were, in case it is needed. One must first act in faith, and the required grace is supplied as needed. North Wind does not want to pamper a coward. "I wasn't brave by myself," Diamond muses. "It was the wind that blew in my face that made me brave." She then explains: "You had to be taught what courage was. You couldn't know what it was without feeling it: therefore, courage was given you. . . . a beginning is the greatest thing of all. To try to be brave is to be brave." To achieve any virtue requires courageously doing it.

That Diamond is made strong by North Wind's blowing in his face suggests that experiencing adversities in a Christian spirit does serve to strengthen a person. "Endurance produces character," Paul observes.[9] One of the reasons why MacDonald in his lectures celebrated the life and poetry of Robert Burns is that he agreed with him on this attitude towards misfortunes:

And, even should misfortunes come,
I here wha sit hae met wi' some, (*who; have*)

An's thanku' for them yet,
They gie the wit of age to youth; (*give; wisdom*)
They let us ken oursel; (*know*)
They make us see the naked truth,
The real guid and ill: (*good*)
Tho losses and crosses
Be lessons right severe
There's wit there, ye'll get there,

---

8. Isa 45:6b–7; Amos 3:6; Rev 15:3–4. For a thorough theological examination of this very challenging issue, see Hart, *The Doors of the Sea.*

9. Rom 5:4.

Ye'll find nae other where.[10] (*not*)

Both authors speak from the reservoirs of their personal experiences.

Diamond's experience in the cathedral is different from what a reader may expect. In chapter 8, Diamond is left alone while the storm rages outside and North Wind performs her unenviable task of sinking the ship. He lies down in front of the huge stained glass window depicting the apostles and falls asleep. In a dream he hears the apostles talking about him and offering surprising opinions. Disgusted at finding Diamond lying there, one remarks: "This is one of North Wind's tricks. . . . I don't understand that woman's conduct. . . . As if we hadn't enough to do with our money, without taking care of other people's children! That's not what forefathers built cathedrals for." The others agree, and proceed to offer further judgments that are far removed from the compassion and concern a person expects from church officials. Even Diamond knows such talk could not come from real apostles.

The passage is shaped by MacDonald's ongoing quarrel with so much that he saw awry in the church of his day, whether that of the dissenters or of the high establishment. He felt a large part of his ministry was to expose such shortcomings and replace them with true Christian principles and attitudes. That these authorities admit they do not at all understand North Wind's conduct and rail against her betrays an immense failure on their part to understand and teach biblical principles. Just as Diamond jumps up and begins to correct them, he awakes to find himself in his hay-loft bed.

Away in the Hyperborean Regions: Chapters 9–11

When Diamond's interest is aroused by a casual remark a clergyman makes about the "back of the north wind," he asks North Wind to take him there. She responds that it would be very difficult for her since she is herself "nobody" there; that is, there is no adversity of any kind in heaven. She adds, "you will be very glad some day to be nobody yourself."

This is a truth at the very heart of Christianity. It depicts the nature of *agape* love, the complete self-giving that is the character of God himself and hence the glad condition of all who share fully in the divine nature. Christian conversion begins with the choosing of Christ over the self, and

10. From "Epistle to David, A Brother Poet," in Knight, ed., *Songs and Poems of Robert Burns.*

Christian character develops as concern for the self decreases and loving service for God and for others grows. Christ states this truth many times, such as when he said "whoever would save his life will lose it, and whoever loses his life for my sake, will save it," and "if any one would come after me, let him deny himself, take up his cross daily, and follow me."[11] Being "nobody someday" depicts that spiritual maturity that all true Christians strive towards in this life but never completely attain. It will be fully realized in the afterlife.

When Diamond is in the throes of a deep, coma-like sleep, North Wind with great difficulty transports him to her doorstep, upon which she sits, depleted of her energies. There are no adversities in the afterlife. She tells him, however, that in order to enter the land behind her back he must pass through her. It is through some adversity—illness or accident—that people pass from this life to the beyond.

At the beginning of chapter 10, the narrator announces his difficulty in describing Diamond's experiences there, both because Diamond could not recall much about them, and because the otherness of the experiences he did recall is so pronounced that he is at a loss to describe them adequately. MacDonald has in mind Paul's remarks that "Eye has not seen, nor ear heard, neither has it entered into the heart of man, what God has prepared for those who love him."[12] Paul had great difficulty himself in speaking about his own experience of being caught up into the "third heaven" because there he "heard things that cannot be told, which man may not utter."[13] That Paul describes his experience in the third person—"I knew a man," he says—suggests the complete change of one's nature that must take place before a person can know the full joy of heaven. Paul assures his readers "we shall all be changed."[14] When Christ spoke of heaven, he did not indulge in description, but rather focused attention upon God, for oneness with God is the requisite and essential condition. Somewhat coyly, MacDonald has his narrator compensate for Diamond's failure to recollect his experience more fully by referring briefly to the works of two other authors, Dante's *Paradiso* in *The Divine Comedy*, and James Hogg's poem "Kilmeny." The many denizens of Dante's heaven are "so free and so just and so healthy, that every one of them has a crown like a king and a

11. Luke 9:23, 24.
12. 1 Cor 2:9.
13. 2 Cor 12:4.
14. 1 Cor 15:51. See this chapter throughout.

mitre like a priest." The Scottish peasant girl Kilmeny "had been she knew not where, / And Kilmeny had seen what she could not declare." In Hogg's poem, however, there is a quantity of description of idyllic nature scenes.

Diamond does have some vague recollections. He remembers a river there, which echoes the psalmist David writing "there is a river whose streams make glad the city of God."[15] The river flows freely over the grass, singing melodiously. It inspires Diamond's many attempts that come later in the story to reproduce what he had heard, songs with enchanting rhythms that border on nonsense. They suggest an existence of transcendent delight just beyond the reach of our temporal imaginations.

However, although the people in the land behind the North Wind's back knew "something better than mere happiness," things were not as right as they one day will be. They await the resurrection and their concomitant reunion with loved ones who have not yet joined them. Diamond recalls seeing there the daughter of the Coleman's gardener, who thought he had lost his child forever. Not so; Diamond is assured she will "come back some day . . . if they would only wait." She will return with Christ at the resurrection.[16] The people there are allowed, nevertheless, to view the activities of those on earth in whom they are interested by climbing a certain tree and watching what they are doing.[17]

Diamond is not contented to stay; he wants to return to his family, and North Wind obliges him. She has, however, to undergo several mutations, gradually changing from being a spider through a succession of more forbidding animals until she becomes a Bengal tiger. The severity of possible adversities increases as the nearer they come to earth. Diamond gradually comes out of his seven-day coma and regains his strength by being given "chicken broth and other nice things."

The suggestion contained in the title of the story has now been fulfilled, but the story itself is but one-third over, and the hurried reader may well wonder why and be impatient with the remainder. A reader's frustration may be increased by noting that the role of North Wind is muted until near the end. But all of MacDonald's purposes in writing are yet to be worked

15. Ps 46:4.

16. 1 Thess 4:14: "For since we believe that Jesus died and rose again, even so, through Jesus God will bring with him those who have died."

17. Heb 21:1: "Therefore, since we are surrounded by so great a cloud of witnesses, let us also lay aside every weight . . ."

out. Positive attitudes toward adversity and the certainty of hope should shape the Christian's everyday life, and he proceeds to illustrate how.

It's all in the Wind: Chapters 12–13

The story now explores the individual and social effects of North Wind's activities—events that may seem to be evil ones in the eyes of uninformed people—and to demonstrate how the potential for good that lies in adversities may be realized within the lives of those affected. A large part of the realization that good flows through the lives of people who serve is shown in the active role Diamond now plays in the lives of others. The attitudes he has learned to hold towards the activities of North Wind, together with his knowledge of the glories of the realm behind her back, provide the motivations for his actions. MacDonald's world is one permeated and controlled by the providence of God, but he certainly does not conclude that a person may therefore simply be a passive observer of God as he in his sovereignty works out his will apart from human instrumentality. God works through his people.

Having returned, Diamond learns that the ship North Wind sank belonged to Mr. Coleman, who is now deep into economic woes. The narrator muses: "It is a hard thing for a rich man to grow poor; but it is an awful thing for him to grow dishonest, and some kinds of speculation lead a man deep into dishonesty before he thinks what he is about. Poverty will not make a man worthless—he may be worth a great deal more when he is poor than he was when he was rich; but dishonesty goes very far indeed to make a man of no value—a thing to be thrown out in the dust-hole of the creation." Economic poverty is a much more fertile soil than economic riches for the growing of spiritual fruit. MacDonald orchestrates this theme throughout his writings.

Human value is achieved through complete trust and virtuous acts. In the dialogue between Diamond and his mother in chapter 13, Diamond is unable to understand his mother's worrisome concerns about their family welfare, now that his father is no longer working for the Coleman's. She sees life as a troublesome affair filled with uncertainties. Diamond counters with attitudes of trust and tranquility, being content with the adequacies of the present and "taking no thought for tomorrow."[18]

---

18. Matt 6:25–33.

When Diamond's mother worries about where their future food and shelter are to come from, he asks if she is hungry right then: if so, there is food in their picnic basket. When her mind dwells upon all the hungry people of world, Diamond observes they will die and pass on to another world "where they get something to eat." To her "petulantly" opining that they may not want what they are given, Diamond responds, "that's all right then." In a quick aside the narrator remarks that he was "thinking, I dare say, more than he chose to put in words."

The narrator's remark suggests much of MacDonald's thought. A person's concern should be for the present moment, regarding the things one can affect, and not regarding that which one cannot. Souls passing into the afterlife exist beyond physical needs; they will be offered that which above all things they need most, a right relationship to their Creator, together with the means of achieving it. Any who refuse must face the inevitable consequences of separation from the very Source and Sustainer of their being.[19]

After mother and son eat their picnic lunch, Diamond rests on the beach and falls into a soporific state in which he hears, to the background of his mother's reading nursery rhymes to him, an extended highly rhythmic poem that sings enchantingly but barely makes sense. It is, Diamond affirms, how the river in the land at the back of the North Wind sounded. This, together with the gist of thought of the entire thirteenth chapter, suggests the transcending otherness of the reality of heaven.

On the Horse's Back with Comb and Brush: Chapters 14–15

MacDonald's thought in this fantasy, however, is focused on the here and now, not—as it is, say, in *Lilith*—upon the afterlife. Chapter 14 is entitled "Old Diamond." In contrast to the symbolic significance of North Wind as the supernatural world beyond man's direct control, the horse symbolizes the natural world of the here and now, a creation provided to people for them to steward and employ for their welfare. The orientation to the supernatural that Diamond has acquired has fitted him to stand in right relationship to the natural and social worlds in which he finds himself.

The image of the horse is prominent in this latter portion of the fantasy, as the image of the wind was in the former. Diamond is most

---

19. "In him we live and move and have our being," Acts 17:28.

contented when he is sitting upon the back of either. The relationship to each is, however, quite different. North Wind is the mysterious "other" to whom obedience, submission, and trust are essential. On the other hand, he must learn to make the horse obedient and submissive to him. He learns to kindly control the horse and care for it, harnessing its energies to fulfill his purposes. In short, he must care for the horse, as North Wind cares for him, and it is crucial to the quality of his life that he maintain a healthy attitude towards each. Were he not to have utter faith in North Wind, or were he to be cruel or neglectful of the horse, his life would be plunged into uncertainty and discontent.

Providentially, although Coleman had to sell the family's beloved horse, Diamond's father is able to retrieve it and try his hand at being a London cabman. The family finds new living quarters in the "mews," or alleyway behind urban residential houses, that accesses the stables and meager living quarters for those who tend the horses.

Diamond immediately assumes a positive attitude towards his new surroundings. The narrator muses: ". . . if he had never been to the back of the north wind, I am afraid he would have cried a little. . . . he began to find out all the advantages of the place; for every place has some advantages, and they are always better worth knowing than the disadvantages." Everything is fraught with potential blessing. Both realms of life—the supernatural and the natural—are sacramental; that is, they both are channels offering grace.

A person's attitudes determine the extent to which the sacramental potential is realized, and a person's attitude has an immense effect upon others. Diamond rises to the challenge. When his parents are "rather miserable," he affirms: "This won't do. I can't give into this. I've been to the back of the north wind. Things go right there, and so I must try to get things to go right here. I've got to fight the miserable things. They won't make me miserable if I can help it." Such is no doubt one of the reasons Christ remarked: "The eye is the lamp of the body. So, if your eye is healthy your whole body will be full of light; but if your eye is unhealthy, your whole body will be full of darkness. If then the light in you is darkness, how great is the darkness."[20] To see the world in the light of the eternal is to shape the nature of how one faces it.

---

20. Matt 6:22–23.

Destroying the Misery: Chapters 16–25

MacDonald wants his readers to contemplate how sacramental grace flows through dedicated lives. He therefore devotes a considerable portion of the fantasy to Diamond's relationship with all with whom he comes into contact. When his father falls ill, Diamond undertakes to drive his father's cab, impressing many with his prowess and winning attitudes. His friendly readiness to be of help to everyone he meets, together with his songs—which appear to many as nonsense, but are remnants of what he remembers of the songs of the angels—transform all the everyday situations in which he is involved, dismissing the gloom.

Most prominent among those affected is the little street sweeper, Nanny. On Diamond's first excursion with North Wind, they observe her sweeping her London street crossing. He immediately wants North Wind to help her, and when she tells him she cannot, but he could, he leaves her to befriend Nanny himself. Why cannot North Wind help Nanny? She is a tough-spirited little girl with a good heart, living in still more deplorable poverty-stricken conditions than Diamond. But she lacks the proper attitude towards the unseen spiritual world: she lacks faith. When Diamond tells her of his experiences, she dismisses them utterly as foolishness.

North Wind asked Diamond: "Do you think if you don't see it happen then nothing is being done?" In the course of the story, Nanny takes seriously ill. Diamond and Mr. Raymond, a kindly gentleman who also is ready and eager to help those in need, get her into a children's hospital. There, through their instrumentality, the effects of her suffering, and her dream while ill (which also is sent by North Wind), she becomes a sweet-tempered girl, and is set on a course that issues in a much more satisfactory life.

Various Shapes for Various People: Chapters 26–36

In the children's hospital Mr. Raymond tells them a story entitled "Little Daylight," which affirms that evil spirits engineer some of the adversities of life. It tells about a princess at whose christening a wicked fairy places a curse upon, to the effect that she must sleep while the sun shines and only be awake at night, her beauty waxing and waning with the moon. The spell may be broken only by the kiss of a prince. A prince from a neighboring realm, disguised as a peasant, wanders into her woods, is charmed when he sees her, and, after considerable heightening of the reader's suspense and expectation, kisses her and the spell is broken.

It is a charming fairy tale whose theme buttresses that of the fantasy at large, that evil serves to enhance the good. The narrator summarizes: "wicked fairies are terribly stupid; even though from the beginning of the world they have really been helping instead of hindering the good fairies, none of them realizes it at all." But in the "real" world of Diamond's adventures, the good that is realized in multiple situations is channeled through his acts and attitudes; the full realization of the good out of evil is dependent upon human instrumentality.

In the hospital, Nanny is given a ruby ring whose color fascinates her and triggers her dream, in which there are a number of red images. Red is also the color of Ruby, the horse that through Mr. Raymond is given to Diamond's father as a test of his integrity. One may recall that the red horse in St. John's apocalyptic visions in the Bible signifies evil, misery, and strife.[21] Again, the basic theme of the fantasy is subtly reinforced.

Nanny's dream takes her through disobedience to repentance, which readies her for a different course in life when she gets well. Diamond's mother takes her into their home and trains her in the arts of housekeeping. The adversity of her illness has generated a turnaround to a promising future. In MacDonald's thinking all such situations have a great potential to convey grace.

Much of the good that occurs in the lives of the different characters introduced into the story—that of the family of the drunken cabman, and of the good that issues in lives of the Coleman family—is achieved through Diamond's ready and cheerful willingness to help others and alleviate any suffering that he sees. In every aspect of life, attitudes of love and concern are channels of grace.

Just before the conclusion of the story, North Wind identifies herself to Diamond: "I don't think I am just what you imagine me to be. I have to shape myself various ways to various people. But the heart of me is true. People call me by terrible names and think they know all about me. But they don't. Sometimes they call me Bad Fortune, sometimes Evil Chance, sometimes Ruin—and they have another name for me that they think the most terrible of all." The other name is, of course, Death.

Why's hasn't MacDonald told the child listener this sooner? Isn't this central to the gist of the story? Yes, considered from an abstract intellectual

21. Rev 6:3.

point of view. But there is another understanding that MacDonald wants to instill within the child, a spiritual, heartfelt one, that is imaginatively achieved. To give Diamond the conventional intellectual understanding before his acquaintance with her has fully assured him of her gracious, loving attitudes and the spiritual purposes she is working to achieve would be to prevent the fairy tale from working its particular magic upon a child. A fairy tale impacts a child not through direct statement nearly so much as through identification with the hero.[22] As much as possible, MacDonald wants to keep at bay as long as he can a purely abstract understanding with all its negative emotional connotations. The best vehicle for saying what he wants to say is the fantasy with its compelling imaginative appeal.

It is the fertile imagination of the child, so receptive to the impact of story, that allows MacDonald to fulfill his purposes. Diamond's visit to the back of the North Wind has made him the incarnation of faith, love, and hope, the essential Christian attitudes.

---

22. "It is not the fact that virtue wins out at the end which promotes morality, but that the hero is most attractive to the child, who identifies with the hero in all his struggles. Because of this identification the child imagines that he suffers with the hero his trials and tribulations, and triumphs with him as virtue is victorious. The child makes such identifications all on his own, and the inner and outer struggles of the hero imprint morality on him." Bruno Bettelheim, *The Uses of Enchantment*, Introduction.

7

The Golden Key

The Borders Of Fairy Land

Grand and strong beyond all that human imagination can conceive of poet-thinking and kingly action, he is delicate beyond all that human tenderness can conceive of husband or wife, homely beyond all that human heart can conceive of father or mother. He has not two thoughts about us. With him all is simplicity of purpose and meaning and effort and end—namely, that we should be as he is, think the same thoughts, mean the same things, possess the same blessedness. It is so plain that any one may see it, everyone ought to see it, everyone shall see it. It must be so. He is utterly true and good to us, nor shall anything withstand his will. "The Child in the Midst," *Unspoken Sermons: Series One.*

*T*he Golden Key first appeared in *Dealings with the Fairies*, which was published in 1867. The volume also contains *The Light Princess*, *The Giant's Heart*, *The Shadows*, and *Cross Purposes*. All of them explore with imaginative verve some aspect of the soul's orientation to spiritual reality. However, *The Golden Key* is the most compelling, its view of life the most comprehensive, and its theological implications the strongest. J. R. R. Tolkien remarks that:

> .... fairy-stories as a whole have three faces: the Mystical towards the Supernatural; the Magical towards Nature; and the Mirror of scorn and pity towards Man. The essential face of Faerie is the middle one, the Magical. But the degree in which the others

appear (if at all) is variable, and may be decided by the individual story-teller. The Magical, the fairy-story, may be used as a *Mirour de l'Omme;* and it may (but not so easily) be made a vehicle of Mystery. This at least is what George MacDonald attempted, achieving stores of power and beauty when he succeeded, as in *The Golden Key.*[1]

This story is a fine example of these "three faces." The presentation of the supernatural inspires mystery and wonder; the depiction of nature has a penetrating charm that casts it in a spiritually convincing light; and the attitude towards the characters, though certainly not one of scorn, is one of sympathy and fascination. Its imaginative power is spellbinding, and its aesthetic impact very satisfying. Its purity, however, makes it the more challenging to articulate an interpretation. In reading it a person feels that it means intensely, but the meaning is chiefly received by the heart, apart from intellectual assimilation. Nevertheless, one ponders it.

The opening image of twilight sets the atmosphere and tone, and the images of the rainbow and the golden key pertain throughout. The subdued light that marks the transition from daylight to darkness is appropriate to the indistinct intellectual import of the main images as well as to the sense of anticipation of that which is to come. The tone of longing and expectation, together with that of rising, is created at the outset and beautifully maintained throughout the tale.

The boy, whose name we later learn is Mossy, lives on the borders of Fairy Land, which, as in all the tales, is the realm of spiritual reality. We are told that the reality of Fairy Land has a permanence that makes that which looks real here "very thin indeed." It is within Fairy Land that the rainbow, with all its breathtaking beauty, can be found. The rainbow recalls God's covenant with man and all living creatures.[2] Here it suggests salvation: when Mossy finds it he sees the forms of "men and women and children—all different, all beautiful" ascending a winding stair in it.

The vision of the rainbow disappears, but on the moss where its base had rested Mossy finds the golden key his great aunt had described. What the key will do Mossy is not told, only that it will unlock a mystery, the discovery of which will make him a happy boy. It is of gold, that is, of great value in itself, and it will admit its owner to something very desirable that

---

1. Tolkien, "On Fairy Stories," *The Tolkien Reader*, 52.
2. Cf. Gen 9:8–17.

must be discovered. Being associated as it is with the aunt's stories and Mossy's aroused curiosity, perhaps one can see it as imaginative faith.

On the borders of Fairy Land as well lives a little girl whose experience of life is greatly different from that of Mossy. She is neglected and abused, the object of the pranks of mischievous fairies. They play tricks upon her and unintentionally frighten her to flee into Fairy Land. When she becomes entrapped in the branches of a tree, a queer creature, an "air-fish," rescues her and leads her to a cottage. The narrator remarks that there are many creatures in Fairy Land, good as well as ill, and the good ones will always help more than the evil ones can harm.

Air-Fish That Want to Be Eaten

Within the cottage lives a beautiful woman. She is an image of the divine presence in life, not unlike that of the great-great-grandmother in the Curdie stories. She lovingly bathes and dresses the girl, whose name is Tangle, and prepares her a meal of the very air-fish that had carefully befriended her. To Tangle's wonder the woman explains that the fish is gladly serving its "highest end"; as soon as it is eaten, out of a pot on the fire a lovely creature arises and flies away.

The imagery is not unlike that of the Curdie stories, in which creatures who have "gone down-hill to the animals' country" are learning the value of obedience and thereby rising to higher forms of life in a universe in which all creatures are ever spiritually becoming, either devolving to lower forms until they acquire wisdom, or else slowly evolving upward to destinies of ineffable glory. It anticipates the collection of grotesque forms that appear in the afterlife portrayed in *Lilith*.

The woman commissions another air-fish to find Mossy and bring him to her cottage as well. Tangle is put to bed, and in the morning she finds herself outside the cottage, having a new understanding of and fascination for the creatures of the woods. In the evening Mossy arrives with the golden key in his hand. Awed by his possessing it, the woman undertakes to serve him, and tells him he must continue to search for the keyhole it will unlock. He and Tangle spend the night with her, and in the morning she sends them on their way together.

Hand in Hand

They leave, hand in hand. As they wander, they are delighted to feel a new-found harmony with the animals of the forest, together with an ability to communicate with them. Squirrels and moles bring them food, while the bees are selfish and rude. But as they proceed, the path becomes steep and treacherous, while for a time darkness thickens. Then they come to an over-look from which they view a green valley and descend into it. They find it filled with lovely shadows, shades of trees and birds, of animals and flowers, and of great variety of people. Momentarily sitting to rest, they find each other in tears, "longing after the country whence the shadows fell." "We *must* find the country from which the shadows come," Mossy declares, and Tangle wonders if his golden key will admit them there. The impress of Plato's myth of the cave with all its implications is strongly upon the scene. This life is one of appearances, the realities of which lie in the world above. Thus imaginatively perceived, the scene has a mythic impact.

They must cross the plain before night to get to their destination. As they proceed through "the constant play of the wonderful shadows," Mossy's hair begins to turn gray, and wrinkles appear on Tangle's brow. Evening draws near, and hand in hand they press onwards "in silence and some dismay." Of a sudden, Tangle loses Mossy's hand, and calling to him, receives no reply.

The passage captures the nature of life at its heart. The couple's leaving the mysterious woman's cottage hand in hand with her blessing suggests their marriage, and passing through the plain of shadows with their mutual experiences is a moving depiction of a loving couple growing old together through all life's happenings and vicissitudes, until the inevitable death of one before the other occurs, with its ensuing loneliness.

Tangle's Journey

Tangle's grief is somewhat assuaged when she remembers that Mossy possessed the golden key. Her decrepitude and death are movingly depicted by her fearfully ascending a mountain, then throwing herself down into the depths of a cave. There she is met by her air-fish, which is now transformed into an aeranth (a being unique to the author's imagination). The aeranth leads her to the Old Man of the Sea and she asks him if he has not some fish ready to be sent to her grandmother. He surveys his great school of fish and concludes none are yet ready. Shades of MacDonald's view of spiritual evolution hover over the episode.

Tangle's motivating desire is to find the way to the country from which the shadows fall. The Old Man of the Sea tells her he does not himself know the way, but he will help her on her journey. Not herself having a golden key, she has many experiences to undergo before she can arrive at her desired destination. First he tells her she must take a bath, which not only renders her more happy and hopeful, but also changes her perception of her host, who now appears to be a grand and majestic man. He sends her on her way to the Old Man of the Earth.

She finds him at the bottom of a seemingly endless winding stair. He appears from behind as an exceedingly old man, but when she sees his face, he appears as a handsome youth. He tells her he too does not know the way, but directs her to proceed to the Old Man of the Fire. Removing a stone from the floor of his cave, he uncovers a deep hole and tells her she must throw herself in: "there is no other way." She feels dismay at the lack of stairs, hesitates, then throws herself headlong into the hole. The image aptly portrays the necessity for, and the nature of, an act of faith.

She finds herself being carried along by a stream of water that takes her into the presence of overwhelming heat. Descending into a cave she sees a little stream, plunges her face into it, drinks, and feels a marvelous sense that

> she was in the secret of the earth and all its ways. Everything she had seen, or learned from books; all that her grandmother had said or sung to her; all the talk of the beasts, birds and fishes; all that had happened to her on her journey with Mossy, and since then in the heart of the earth with the Old man and the Older man—all was plain: she understood it all, and saw that everything meant the same thing, though she could not have put it into words again.

As she turns, she sees a little naked child playing with balls of various sizes and colors, arranging them in patterns of infinite meaning. She feels "there was something in her knowledge which was not in her understanding." She has arrived at the very heart of meaning, the secret of the universe.

The balls remind Tangle of the Valley of Shadows through which she and Mossy passed. Summoning the courage to ask the child where the Old Man of the Fire is, he rises and responds, "Here I am." The words echo God's words as he identifies himself to Abraham, or his words to Moses from the burning bush.[3] The description that follows displays at its height MacDonald's ability to offer to his readers a mythic moment:

> There was such an awfulness of absolute repose on the face of the child that Tangle stood dumb before him. He had no smile, but the love in his large gray eyes was deep as the centre. And with the repose there lay on his face a shimmer as of moonlight, which seemed as if any moment it might break into such a ravishing smile as would cause the beholder to weep himself to death. But the smile never came, and the moonlight lay there unbroken. For the heart of the child was too deep for any smile to reach from it to his face.

Thus MacDonald presents one of his most deeply held convictions, that God the Father, the Creator and Sustainer of the universe, whose nature is a consuming fire because he will achieve moral purity throughout all his creation, is at the same time as tender and as simple in "purpose and meaning and effort and end" as a little child. He is challenging the most prevalent conception of the nature of God held by philosophers, theologians, and teachers—one of grandiose majesty and dictatorial authority—with an image that, posed as it is in a fairy tale, is cunningly shielded against intellectual assault. But it can have a powerful effect upon people who, themselves childlike, read with their imaginations. They are like Tangle who "stood looking for a long time, for there was fascination in the sight; and the longer she looked the more an indescribable vague intelligence went on rousing itself in her mind."

Mossy's Journey

Mossy's journey is similar to Tangle's, but much less stressful, as he has the golden key. After leaving the land of shadows, he arrives at a seashore, and there he sees the Old Man of the Sea, not as Tangle did, but as a "strong kingly man of middle age." Mossy also is led to a bath, and when he arises from it, all signs of old age are gone. Mossy is told he has tasted death, and when he exclaims "It is better than life," he is told "No, it is only more life."

Mossy is then sent upon his way across a stormy sea, but he finds he can now walk on water. As he presses on towards the distant rainbow the storm gives way to lovely weather. Led to a precipice and halfway up, the path stops and he is puzzled as to what to do until he espies a keyhole, tries

---

3. Cf. Gen 22:1; Exod 3:4.

his key and is at once admitted. Stones fall before his feet making a stairway up which he climbs to enter a hallway composed of brilliant, multicolored stones. Ahead he sees Tangle awaiting his arrival.

Their reunion is ecstatic as they share their many experiences and admire each other's newfound youth and beauty. They are "younger and better, and stronger and wiser, than they had ever been before."

Consumed with the desire to press on to the country from which the shadows fall, and searching for a way, they find themselves surrounded by mesmerizing colors and realize they are within the rainbow. The golden key admits them to a winding stair, up which they begin to climb. "Stairs beside stairs wound up together, and beautiful beings of all ages climbed along with them."

Having created the desire within the reader to arrive at the distant country from which the shadows fall, MacDonald is careful to close the tale without any attempt to describe this destination. The ending combines a sense of expectation and intense desire with one of satisfying acceptance. The strong implication is that the destination is quite beyond the reach of the imagination. The conclusion reinforces Paul's assertion: "What no eye has seen, nor ear heard, nor the heart of man imagined, what God has prepared for those who love him."[4]

4. Cf. 1 Cor 2:9.

8

Lilith

George MacDonald's *Lilith* is a challenging work. A good part of the fascinated bepuzzlement one feels in struggling to discern the meanings invested in the various images of *Lilith* arises from the difficulties MacDonald faced when he undertook to convey his worldview while at the same time trying to avoid any trace of mechanical allegory.

If one desires a deeper understanding of the fantasy, it helps to know something of MacDonald's intentions. During the five-year period in which he was writing and rewriting it, G. P. Putnam's Sons of New York, who was preparing a new edition of his fairy tales, asked him for a preface, and in obliging them he made explicit his view of the nature of fairy tales and how they convey meaning.

While refusing to offer a definition of the genre, he committed himself to say "some things helpful to the reading, in right-minded fashion, of such fairy tales as I would wish to write, or care to read." He continued, "It cannot help having some meaning," but "one man will read one meaning in it, another will read another. . . . A genuine work of art must mean many things; the truer its art, the more things it will mean." The imaginative reaches of such works invest them with a richness of implication, so that a range of interpretations is legitimate.

A basic reason why he emphasizes the multiplicity of meaning is that MacDonald felt strongly that each reader is at a different phase in that spiritual journey which all people are on, either progressing or retrogressing, according to how each is responding to whatever may be occurring in their lives. Wherever one is contributes strongly to the meaning that person sees in any of the events that befall, whether in real life or in imaginative stories. A basically good person sees a basically good world; an evil person an evil one.[1]

He therefore intends not to foist his own meanings upon the reader in any pedantic or arbitrary fashion: "A fairytale is not an allegory. There may be allegory in it, but it is not an allegory. He must be an artist indeed who can, in any mode, produce a strict allegory that is not a weariness to the spirit. An allegory must be Mastery or Moorditch."[2]

All this being the case, together with the fact that he intended *Lilith* to be his masterpiece, how is he to give consummate expression to that worldview that he formed early in his career and held with deep conviction throughout his life? "The best thing you can do for your fellow," he concludes, "next to rousing his conscience, is—not to give him things to think about, but to wake things up that are in him; or say, to make him think things for himself." This caveat, then, gives us a solid clue as to how he is performing the very difficult task of not writing allegory but at the same time giving final expression to his life's work. He tried to give us things to think about.

It also helps us understand why there are five distinct and complete versions of the text (all contained in the variorum edition), which he labored over during a five-year period, making a multitude of additions, deletions, and emendations.[3] The task he set for himself was immensely difficult; the fact that *Lilith* continues to be read and puzzled over, with a variety of legitimate reactions, is itself a vindication of his accomplishment.

Anyone, therefore, who would undertake an explanation of this or any of MacDonald's fantasies would do well to keep in mind his strong denial that any given exposition is final. All that having been acknowledged, the temptation to share what one sees in *Lilith* is strong, especially if one is convinced that the fantasy is a very worthy work of art in its genre, and that it does contain a great deal of truth. Such is the case with the present writer.

In short, MacDonald avoids creating a brackish stream (moorditch) of rigid abstract meanings by keeping an engaging narrative salient, with numerous scenes that have no symbolic purpose but exist simply to carry the tale forward. Abstract truths are adumbrated only in certain select scenes.

1. Cf. Ps 18:24–26.
2. Hein, ed., *The Heart of George MacDonald*, 426.
3. Hein, ed., *Lilith: Variorum Edition*.

Also, any given image may suggest differing symbolic implications in different instances, and invariably faintly. The raven, for instance, is at times simply a bird, at others an ancient librarian, and at still others, Adam. The image with the richest variety of meanings is Lilith, who symbolizes evil in its many expressions, sometimes the spirit of materialism, at other times the depraved self, and at still others the range of troubling consequences that evil conduct generates.

The constant temptation is to wring from the text every ounce of allegorical value, and the result, if one is not careful, is serious distortion. One has to allow the text to fulfill itself simply as a fairy tale. But, bringing to it a knowledge of MacDonald's system of thought, and noting the aura that certain images do emit, together with the explanations of the raven, one can arrive at a satisfying and edifying understanding of MacDonald's thought.

Although it may not be apparent at first, MacDonald's understanding of the nature of spiritual reality is in many instances quite in accord with Dante's as expressed in *The Divine Comedy*. That he held Dante's work in highest esteem is abundantly evident from the references to it in his various novels, as well as in the five distinct drafts of *Lilith* which he labored upon during the five-year period prior to its publication. MacDonald may have felt *Lilith* to be a modern imaginative recasting of the spiritual truths that shaped Dante's work, with one noted exception.

Engraved upon the lintel above the gateway to Dante's hell is the somber dictum: "Abandon all hope, you who enter here." MacDonald disagreed. He felt that there is hope for all peoples, and that the biblical basis for that hope is explicit.[4] But, as he makes quite clear in this imaginative rendition of his theological scheme, individual souls must face the severe consequences of all the acts of their former lives, turn from them in complete repudiation, turn to God, be reconciled with all whom they wronged, and then receive their true selves. All depends upon the eventual free-will decision to turn to God. This process may require eons, but God, MacDonald affirmed elsewhere, has a luxurious attitude towards time.

In short, *Lilith* is about what it really means to be born again: its necessity, the various hindrances in the psyche that impede the process, and its glorious outcome. MacDonald's interpretation of this essential Christian experience, however, differs appreciably from the popular understanding of it. It is crucial that each reader approach the text with an open mind and thoroughly understand it before deciding on its orthodoxy. Greville,

---

4. E.g., Isa 45:18–25; Ps 22:27–31; 86:8–10; Rom 11:32; 2 Pet 3:9.

MacDonald's son, remarks in the family biography that when his father began writing he felt he had a "mandate direct from God, for which he himself was to find form and clothing."[5]

MacDonald is offering an interpretation of several biblical principles. In the well-known passage in the Gospel of John, Christ tells Nicodemus that being born again is a necessity. Later he tells his disciples, "If anyone would come after me, let him deny himself and take up his cross and follow me. For whoever would save his life will lose it, but whosoever loses his life for my sake and the gospel's will save it," and "Truly, truly, I say to you, unless a grain of wheat falls into the earth and dies, it remains alone; but if it dies, it bears much fruit." Paul summarizes his own experience by affirming, "I have been crucified with Christ. It is no longer I who live, but Christ who lives in me. And the life I now live in the flesh I live by faith in the Son of God, who loved me and gave himself for me."[6] On the basis of these truths Paul instructs his readers to continually put to death the deeds of their former selves. MacDonald undertakes to give imaginative expression to what these truths mean in human experience.

While no direct mention is made of Christ or God until the denouement of the fantasy, much of the imagery echoes biblical metaphors. The presence of Adam and Eve, of course, should rivet our attention upon the biblical account of the fall. While Lilith is not present in that account, she is very much present in attendant Jewish mythology. Allusions to water echo Christ's identifying himself as the living water of life, and the biblical references to the water of the Word. The numerous allusions to the moon in the text strongly suggest the providential concern and care of God, and the occasional appearance of the sun his more immediate presence.

The Library: Chapter 1

Our protagonist is a young Oxford graduate who has newly arrived to take possession of his inherited ancestral home. We are not told that his name is Mr. Vane until later, but the implications of both pride and futility are quite evident in his opening description of himself. His given name in an earlier manuscript is Fane, which suggests pretense, and he is soon told that he has no idea who he really is at heart. That Vane is preoccupied with "strange analogies" between the physical sciences and "metaphysical facts," and that

5. Greville MacDonald, *George MacDonald and His Wife*, 548.

6. Cf. John 3:3; Mark 8:34, 35; John 12:24; Gal 2:20.

this penchant causes him to fall into "metaphysical dreams," prepares us for all the fantasies of the afterlife that form the text ahead.

Much of the story that is to come concerns the interpenetrating relationship between the natural and the spiritual worlds. The epigraph from Thoreau's essay "Walking" anticipates this concern, and the poetic stanza in chapter 29 underscores this underlying theme, together with affirming the necessity for privileging spiritual reality:

> Ah, the two worlds! So strangely are they one,
> And yet so measurelessly wide apart!
> Oh, had I lived the bodiless alone
> And from defiling sense held safe my heart,
> Then had I scaped the canker and the smart,
> Scaped life-in-death, scaped misery's endless moan!

The early part of the fantasy devotes much space to describing the library in which Vane spends much of his time. He is given to study, and the activity of reading is a catalyst that activates his imagination and nurtures his "metaphysical dreams." One day while situated in his library, he begins to catch fleeting glimpses of an aged man among the stacks, and this, together with the recurring absence and subsequent reappearance of a certain volume in which he is interested, prompts him to question his butler, who affirms that the library is haunted by a former librarian, a Mr. Raven who served Vane's ancestor, Sir Upward.

A Door In: Chapters 2–3

Some weeks later, Vane, again catching a glimpse of the fleeting figure, follows it out of the library, up a flight of stairs, along a wide corridor, up more stairs, and through more passageways to find himself in the garret, a place which he had never before explored. Approaching there a large mirror, he is intrigued to see it reflecting a lovely countryside, and stepping closer, he stumbles over a threshold to find himself in another world and face to face with "a large and ancient raven." Panic-stricken, Vane desperately tries to orient himself to his fantastic surroundings and is astounded to find the raven not only able to talk but also to issue instructions.

We later learn that the raven—an image suggesting death[7]—is also Adam; this suggests that death is the entry into life, which is the kernel

---

7. E.g., cf. Edgar Allan Poe's "The Raven," published in 1845.

idea of *Lilith*. That Vane spends much of his time reading in his old library and discovers the world of spiritual reality by following an ancient librarian suggests that it is in the older writers—rather than Vane's contemporary ones—that a person is most likely to make such a discovery.

One of MacDonald's strengths in creating fantasies is the smooth transitions he is able to effect from this world to the higher, making it quite plausible, and this is a fine example. The narrative acquires the nightmarish quality in which anything can happen, according to laws invented by the fantasist, so long as such laws are consistent with themselves, and no moral law is violated.

The question with which the raven poses to Vane— "who are you, if you happen to know"—introduces one of the chief themes of the fantasy: the nature of the self. Vane is perplexed to be unable to tell the raven who he really is, and the raven presses him with the necessity of becoming his true self, for as it is he is nobody. "In fact, nobody is himself, and himself is nobody, " the raven explains. All of Vane's adventures that follow proceed from this need to find one's true being.

The raven disappears, and Vane, horror-stricken, returns to his garret in a manner that echoes the experience Thoreau described in the epigraph, that of passing through a wood during the gloom of twilight.

Somewhere or Nowhere: Chapters 4–5

In spite of the fact that, after his initial contact with the spiritual realm he had vowed never again to return to that region, Vane has two experiences that belie his determination and suggest how that realm keeps beckoning. The first occurs the evening after his return when he opens a book and ponders some lines of poetry. He muses that the words "woke in me feelings which to describe was, from their strangeness, impossible. Some dreams, some poems, some musical phrases, some pictures, wake feelings such as one never had before . . . spiritual sensations, as it were."

The second occurs when the following morning he is momentarily enthralled with a natural scene. The sun is shining brightly, and as Vane gazes out upon a rain-enlivened lawn he sees the raven approaching him. After having been enticed into the yard, Vane's curiosity is aroused as he watches the raven plunge his beak into the turf, extract a worm, toss it into the air, to see it spread wings and fly away a gorgeous butterfly.

The point is that the world of spiritual reality is persistently trying to summon people's attention, their determination to ignore or deny it notwithstanding. All resistance is futile; to disregard it is to make a fool of oneself. To find the correct orientation to it is necessary to begin to become an individual, to find one's true self.

The raven tells Vane they should be "going where we have to go," and when Vane resists, he is told his reluctance really does not matter: his going is ultimately inevitable. The transformation of worm into butterfly has illustrated the divine principle that, one way or another, in this world or perhaps in a myriad of ages in the next—it may be in times of great suffering—all people will find their way home.

The raven tells Vane that the world into which he is being taken is "the region of seven dimensions," that is, the world of spirit, which is coincident with that of the afterlife. Like the world in which we find ourselves, it is imaginatively received.

In his essay on the imagination, MacDonald remarks: "For the world is—allow us the homely figure—the human being turned inside out."[8] The world that each individual sees is a projection of that individual's thought and nature. And all the images that the mind receives are images of that which God has imagined forth and are sustained by his thinking. An evil nature tends to invest all the images it receives with evil meanings and hence sees an evil world. But a good person sees a good world, and a person in tune with the will of God perceives at least something of the thoughts of God.

The imagined world which we enter in *Lilith*, therefore, is the world shaped by the nature of Vane's own mind, since he is the narrator, and all of its characters and adventures are those most appropriate for his individual condition and needs. The world of the spirit and the afterlife is a world of seven dimensions; the four added to the familiar three—height, depth, and length—are peculiar to the world of the imagination.

It is tempting to surmise that these added dimensions are the same as Dante had in mind when he explained the several levels of meaning resident in his allegorical work, *The Divine Comedy*. In a letter written to his patron, Can Grande della Scala, he remarks that in his allegory he intends four levels of meaning, which he terms the literal, the allegorical, the moral, and the anagogical.[9] While it may be difficult and perhaps unnecessary to parse

8. Hein, ed., *The Heart of George MacDonald*, 418.
9. Sayers, ed., *Comedy*, 14–15.

these distinct meanings in any specific episode, the obvious implication is that an image in a fantasy may have a richness in allegorical intention. The emphasis at some times may fall on one aspect of its significance, and at other times on another. There are moments in which a specific allegorical intention is evident, but those same allegorical values may not be sustained throughout the text. We will see how this plays out when we consider the allegorical meanings of Lilith herself.

The raven continues to explain to Vane that all objects in the world we know have their counterpart in the world of spirit: music here may appear as beautiful flowers there, prayers rising like white pigeons, etc. The chapter closes with Vane adopting a positive attitude toward this world in which he must make himself at home, and he agrees that the raven take him to his wife.

The Sexton's Cemetery: Chapters 6–7

Vane, therefore, becomes a pilgrim not unlike Dante in *The Divine Comedy*. Both journey through the afterworld, learning there the truths of spiritual reality. These truths should be implemented in this life to the degree they can be, and will most certainly be fully realized in the life to come.

The raven introduces Vane to his wife, who bids him welcome and invites him to sleep in their "cemetery." She is compared to Beatrice, Dante's beloved who in *The Divine Comedy* introduces him to heaven; so she is beckoning Vane to the possibility of his entering a fully redeemed state. This is one of the two references to Dante that remain in the published text; as we have remarked earlier, there are a great many allusions to Dante's work in the earlier manuscripts. MacDonald is here signaling his affinity with Dante's great poem, but is being careful not to suggest too great a reliance upon that work. The wife's dazzling splendor reflects that of the fully redeemed self; her abode is the vestibule to Paradise.

Vane, however, wants rather to return a "do a day's work first"; that is, he is possessed of the common misconception that it is by good works that one makes oneself worthy of life eternal. The sexton's wife observes that he has first to learn that "the day begins with sleep"; that is, complete death to the self, which is the essence of Christian conversion.

Vane is both curious and repelled as he is shown the innumerable couches upon which silent forms recline. The light of the moon pervades the silent chamber. But when the sexton kindly urges him to commit himself to the couch reserved for him, he adamantly refuses and, panic-stricken, flees and finds himself returned to his library. Searching there for a book, he comes upon an old manuscript in his father's writing, and sits down to read.

My Father's Manuscript: Chapter 8

In his manuscript the father has left a record of his own encounter with the raven, emphasizing the truth that the journey into the world of spirit is an inner journey, an imaginative delving into the human heart. "A book is a door in, and therefore a door out," the raven explains, that is, out of this world of space and time and into the imaginative reaches of the mind. In answer to the father's remark that "things in that world are not things to have and to hold" the raven replies: "Think a little farther; did anything ever become yours, except by getting into that world?" One may think of Christ's admonishment that we should lay up treasures in heaven, for only what is deposited there is eternally ours.

Vane Repents: Chapter 9

Encouraged by learning of his father's experience, Vane is emboldened to return to the Raven's region and accept the invitation to sleep in their abode, but alas, after he returns, the raven refuses to take him. Why so? Because of Vane's motivation: he sees himself as on a fact-finding mission. He now regrets that formerly he had refused an opportunity to gather so much knowledge about the experience.

When Vane asks to be shown the "nearest way home," the raven confronts him with a seemingly impossible quandary: he cannot give him directions, "But you will get there; you must get there; you have to get there. Everybody who is not at home, has to go home."

Vane must learn that his going home will not be by way of rational analysis and intellectual understanding. He is like most people who, when confronting spiritual reality, want to give it careful intellectual consideration. The chapter closes with his honest consideration of his struggle, quite aware of his inclination towards "metaphysical argument," and reluctantly realizing he can explain his experiences only by affirming his feelings and his imaginative perceptions. "It is God who gives you your mirror of imagination, and if you keep it clean, it will give back no shadow but of the truth," MacDonald asserts in *Paul Faber, Surgeon.*[10]

The Bad Burrow: Chapter 10

Vane's experience at the beginning of this chapter graphically illustrates his dilemma. A gorgeous bird-butterfly appears hovering above him and, feeling that if only he could have it in his hands the "treasure of the universe" would be his. In other words, he wants to grasp the experience intellectually, to understand it. But the instant he has it in his hand, "its light went out, all was dark as pitch." MacDonald is making a crucial point: rational analysis of imaginative perceptions of truth tend to kill them. John Masefield speaks of

> That frost of fact by which our wisdom gives
> Correctly stated death to all that lives.[11]

This is certainly not to say that a clear intellectual understanding of basic theological truths is not essential and to be sought, but it is to acknowledge the very important truth that the nature of Ultimate Reality is quite beyond the ability of the rational mind fully to grasp. Were it not so, the human mind could subsume God, making itself in effect a god. The intellect and the imagination must work in tandem. MacDonald explains:

> There were no imagination without our intellect, however much it may appear that intellect can exist without imagination. What we mean to insist upon is, that in finding out the words of God, the Intellect must labour, workman-like, under the direction of the architect, Imagination.[12]

When the intellect acknowledges that the imagination has an indispensable role in one's quest for understanding, a person finds the proper orientation to the mysteries of life.

Vane presses on through the Bad Burrow, following the progress of the moon across the sky. Quite often in MacDonald's writings the moon suggests the mystery of divine providence, and so here. It brings him light, we are told, but no definite guidance; nevertheless, it protects him from the

10. Chapter 29.
11. Masefield, *Poems*, 192.
12. Hein, ed., *The Heart of George MacDonald*, 419.

monsters that menacingly spring up around him. He must himself choose his way. It is in this burrow that he catches the first glimpse of Lilith, whom he sees disintegrating before his eyes, her arms and legs fleeing in the form of serpents and bats.

The Evil Wood: Chapter 11

The Evil Wood has been defined for us earlier by the raven: "It is the place where those who will not sleep, wake up at night, to kill their dead and bury them." It is, in short, an inner journey, a journey through a world uniquely shaped by the specific spiritual needs of any given traveler.

MacDonald made his thinking on the nature of the "outer darkness" clear in a preface he wrote some ten years earlier to *Letters from Hell*, an anonymous volume by a Danish author that was exceedingly popular in the later half of the nineteenth century. He affirmed:

> . . . the awful verity, that we make our fate in unmaking ourselves; that men, in defacing the image of God in themselves, construct for themselves a world of horror and dismay; that of the outer darkness our own deeds and character are the informing or inwardly creating cause; that if a man will not have God, he never can be rid of his weary and hateful self.[13]

By their unrighteous acts people are not only defacing the image of God within them in this life; their acts have ongoing consequences that shape that world of the mind into which they enter beyond the grave, a world that is uniquely of their own making.

Vane's "Evil Wood" is, therefore, an imaginative projection of his inner being. It is an arid desert, made so by his prevailing egoism and exclusive intellectuality. He is haunted by sounds of flowing waters beneath the surface—spiritual truths, though not totally absent and unavailable, are not his conscious concern; hence, they are not immediately available to him. He must first "kill his dead, and bury them."

Vane comes upon multitudes engaged in a "furious battle" in which "curses and credos, snarls and sneers, laughter and mockery, sacred names and howls of hate" fill the air. "The holiest words went with the most hating blow" while howls of "*The Truth! The Truth*" rise above the rage. "None stooped to comfort the fallen, or stepped wide to spare him." Such are the

---

13. Preface, *Letters from Hell*, vi.

sectarian fights over non-essentials—affairs created by exclusively intellectual concerns and overriding self-centeredness, conducted utterly apart from the Christian spirit of love and peace. Such has been so much of the history of the Christian church. But the essential point for Vane is that he is viewing a scene that is what it is because it is motivated by the tendencies of his own personality. He is seeing the result of lives that have given priority to self-interest and who see life only in barren intellectual terms.

Urging on the combatants is the image of a woman: Lilith. She here symbolizes overarching egoism. Her symbolic significance will become clearer when we see her later in the text. Viewing that melee, Vane's own intense egoism is moderated: he now feels a desire for some communion with some "human presence."

Friends and Foes: Chapters 12–13

Vane's desire for some fellowship with fellow beings is met by his meeting the Little Ones, a group that stands in marked contrast to that of the prior chapter. Their spirit of joyous innocence epitomizes the beginning of the spiritual ideal of receiving a new self. They embody the positive traits of children, those that Christ had in mind when he told his disciples that unless they become like little children, they will not enter the kingdom of God. The new birth has begun in them. The Little Ones, therefore, seem to symbolize the true church on earth. They stand in vivid contrast to the melee above overseen by Lilith. That Vane responds to their antics with interest and delight augurs well for his spiritual progress.

Vane's mirthful interaction with such innocence and naivety, however, soon changes into dismay, as he is met and overpowered by some giants, beings that typify malice and greed. Each was once among the Little Ones. The history of the church is plagued by those that were once converts but were seized by various vices and became the church's greatest enemies. That Vane is momentarily held captive by such beings indicates his own tendencies toward the traits that shape their gianthood. But his chief desire is for the society of the Little Ones.

Among the Little Ones is a queen-mother figure named Lona; she signifies the good that comes from evil, as will become clearer later. Lona finds babies in the woods and nurses them into the carefree and joyous state of the Little Ones, but with a wary eye lest they turn into one of the giants. Adversities in life are among the prime motivators for people to become

Christians and to maintain Christian commitment. Lona explains: "The giants were not made always. If a Little One doesn't care, he grows greedy, and then lazy, and then big, and then stupid, and then bad." Lona and Vane watch the process work itself out in Blunty.

A Crisis: Chapter 14

Although Vane feels an attraction to the spiritual state of the Little Ones, his refusal to have slept in the sexton's house signals his need to undergo further conditioning. It takes the form of his mistaken effort to improve their lot. He purposes to help them grow and develop into a yet higher state. For this he determines to leave and search for more knowledge of their nature, history, and destiny.

Vane's ambition precipitates the incidents that next befall him: a momentary run-in with a Giant, together with a future sojourn in the "Cat-woman's" house. The moon, God's providence, appears—as Lona remarks—"to take care of you, and show you the way," and he embarks, but not without a certain misgiving as to the possible effects of his intentions. The chapter closes with a very wise dictum: "The part of philanthropist is indeed a dangerous one, and the man who would do his neighbour good must first study how not to do him evil, and must begin by pulling out the beam from his own eye."

A Strange Hostess: Chapter 15

The providence of God—the moon—leads Vane next to an encounter with the feared Cat-woman, who bids him follow her to her house. The theme of personal identity dominates the chapter. She is reluctant to tell Vane her name, saying, "When you know me, call me by the name that seems to you to fit me, that will tell me what sort you are." Later she identifies herself as Mara, which is a biblical name translated "bitter." In the book of Ruth, Naomi changes her name to Mara because of the suffering she has endured. After their crossing of the Red Sea, the Israelites come upon a fountain of brackish water named Marah. Allegorically, therefore, Mara is adversity.

In his writings MacDonald often makes a point of the function of adversity in the formation of character. He muses: "So sure am I that many things which illness has led me to see are true, that I would endlessly rathernever be well than lose sight of them."[14] Vane cannot at first see Mara's face; that is, perceive her true character. Later when he does glimpse it, he sees her indescribable beauty. Her role in the formation of one's true character is indispensable.

Here and elsewhere MacDonald's thought is shaped by the Augustinian concept of *felix culpa,* the fortunate fall. A fallen world is necessary for the production of virtue. The poet Edwin Muir muses:

> What had Eden ever to say
> Of hope and faith and pity and love,
> Until was buried all its day
> And memory found its treasure trove?
> Strange blessings never in Paradise
> Fall from these beclouded skies.[15]

All the adversities of life issue from the fall; to receive them rightly and allow them to accomplish their all-important work of producing hope, faith, pity, and love, is to achieve one's true name, that is, one's divinely ordained character. Mara tells Vane, who cannot recall his own name: "Your real name, indeed is written on your forehead, but at present it whirls about so irregularly that nobody can read it. I will do my part to steady it." There are echoes here of Christ's telling St. John: "To the one who conquers I will give some of the hidden manna, and I will give him a white stone, with a new name written on the stone that no one knows except the one who receives it."[16]

We learn later in the text that Mara's house necessarily stands between the Evil Wood and Eve's house of sleep. Those who will not sleep in Eve's house must inevitably spend time in Mara's before being given a second chance. One may recall James's admonition to receive trials with joy, or Paul's remark to the Romans that he rejoiced in his sufferings.[17]

We are further prepared for eventually meeting Lilith when Mara describes her as the ruling princess of the city of Bulika, the incarnation of materialism. The pun on "bulk" summarizes the true worth of all the city epitomizes. The country, that was formerly the Land of Waters, is now an arid desert, as Lilith has evicted from the city all spiritual concerns; still,

---

14. *Paul Faber, Surgeon,* chapter 36.

15. Muir, "One Foot in Eden," in *Collected Poems,* 89.

16. Rev 2:17.

17. Jas 1:2; Rom 5:3.

they do flow far underground. Sacramental energies are still present, but faintly so; materialist preoccupations are directly opposed to them.

A Gruesome Dance: Chapter 16

The chapter begins with Vane's asserting the basic principle of life that will shape all the adventures that are to come: "That which is within a man, not that which lies beyond his vision, is the main factor in what is about to befall him." He further explains: "The operation upon him is the event. Foreseeing is not understanding," that is, the spiritual effectiveness of an event depends upon the attitudes with which a person receives it and the actions that proceed from it, not simply upon one's intellectual grasp of it. Until he acts appropriately, he realizes: *everywhere* was the same as *nowhere*. "I had not yet, by doing something in it, made *anywhere* into a place!" That his actions, however, must be shaped by obedience to divine commands and not simply by his self-generated intentions, he has yet to learn.

Vane begins to long to meet other beings. He muses, "I began to learn that it was impossible to live for oneself even, save in the presence of others—then alas, fearfully possible! Evil was only through good! selfishness but a parasite on the tree of life!" The presence of others is essential for spiritually meaningful actions; virtue is generated only in relationships.

Relaxing upon an evening in a great castle, Vane is awakened at midnight to see a host of richly attired men and women caught up in the dances of life. Upon closer look he sees that all were skeletons without faces—only "lidless, living eyes." Such is worldly society, it is implied: its pressures toward conformity eviscerate individuality. They are "condemned to go without faces until they repented." Moving among them Vane is utterly ignored; his loneliness increases.

Very similar to the goddess who rules over Bulika, a woman overlooks the crowd with scorn, embodying the spirit that possesses them all. Suddenly, she cries out in pain, pressing a dark shadow on her side, and flees. With her absence, the crowd of skeletons experiences "a flash of joy" and decaying flesh is shed from their bones. She is Lilith.

Here is a prime example of how MacDonald invests certain of his key images with symbolic value and at the same time avoids the more mechanical aura of pure allegory: the image of Lilith conveys differing (although related) meanings in different situations. We have glimpsed her now three times in the text, and each time she has represented a variation of evil.

Evil is, of course, multi-faceted. In her first appearance in the Bad Burrow she appears as a beautiful woman with a dark spot by her heart that she clutches, writhing in pain. Her body then disintegrates, and her various organs disappear. She epitomizes evil, and evil has within itself the seeds of its own destruction. Like the proverbial calf, give it rope enough and it will hang itself. The frequent references to the spot on her side is a constant reminder of this truth.

When Lilith appears as the princess ruling over Bulika, she symbolizes the ruling spirit of materialism, which is another embodiment of evil. And as she gloatingly lords it over the crowd without faces, she represents the very essence of self-centeredness, the depraved self. That is the curse that isolates each skeleton and prevents them from growing faces.

A Grotesque Tragedy: Chapter 17

Vane oversees a couple of skeletons spitefully railing upon each other, but who, nevertheless, extend a modicum of help or sympathy each to the other. In answer to Vane's questioning—"What can come of it? These are too wretched for any world, and this cannot be hell, for the Little Ones are in it, and the sleepers too!"—the raven appears to explain that Vane is not in hell but the two skeletons are. Hell is a condition of the mind possessed of exclusive self-concern. His explanation conveys much of MacDonald's theology: "they must at last grow weary of their mutual repugnance, and begin to love one another, for love, not hate, is deepest in what Love 'loved into being.'"

That no mention is made of their individual transgressions, as in Dante's *Divine Comedy*, for instance, indicates that God is not interested in punishment for punishment's sake; forgiveness is universal, but it is not effective for an individual until it is accepted. Souls must reject their former selves and then acquire new selves possessed of love.

The raven leaves Vane with a principle upon which he must act: "In this world, never trust a person who has once deceived you. Above all, never do anything such a one may ask you to do." Vane's obedience or dis-obedience will determine what will next befall him.

Lilith Encountered: Chapters 18–25

Over the next several chapters the narrative proceeds with a minimum of allegorical intent. That the moon seems disturbed as Vane goes on his way suggests he is about to make a misstep. Coming upon an emaciated, seemly comatose body of a woman, he painstakingly tries to revive her, with gradual success. But during his efforts he experiences nocturnal blood-sucking visits that debilitate him. And when she is revived, she treats him scornfully, deceiving him by saying she caught a "great white leech" that was biting him while he slept, when in reality it is she who is acting as a vampire, sucking his blood. After another of her attacks, she disappears. Enfeebled, he nevertheless pursues her, convinced against all evidence that she possesses a higher beauty that is "profoundly hidden."

While the narrative through these chapters is salient, one important allegorical value is strongly present. Vane is, remember, in his "outer darkness," where his "own deeds and character are the informing and inwardly creating cause." In nursing Lilith Vane is in short nurturing his depraved self; the fallen self is another object that evil permeates in a fallen world. When Vane undertook his mission to learn more about the Little Ones, rather than to sleep in Eve's house, he pitched his judgment against that of the raven. Preferring one's own judgment over obedience to the demands of moral and spiritual reality is the essence of human depravity. His fascination with Lilith's beauty suggests his growing love for himself—a willingness to trust his own judgment. The debilitating leech bites suggest the steady spiritual diminishment of one's true being that results from loving and pampering the self, rather than denying its base desires.

In the character of Lilith, MacDonald is making a strong statement against all self-interest and egoism as the motivation for action. One recalls Christ's saying, "If any man would come after me, let him deny himself and take up his cross and follow me. For whoever would save his life will lose it, and whosoever loses his life for my sake will find it." By self-denial MacDonald is careful to make the point that he does not mean a person should deny oneself pleasurable activities, nor is he advocating some psychological effort independent from divine help. There are forms of self-denial that but feed pride and self-esteem. Rather, the self must be surrendered entirely to the rule of God. Elsewhere he writes:

> From a man's rule of himself, in smallest opposition, however devout, to the law of his being, arises the huge danger of nourishing,

by the pride of self-conquest, a far worse than even the unchained animal self—the demoniac self. True victory over self is the victory of God in the man, not of the man alone. . . . In whatever man does without God, he must fail miserably—or succeed more miserably.[18]

As the narrative of *Lilith* progresses, MacDonald continues to employ this symbolic level to make his thought abundantly clear.

At one point Vane sees a white leopardess with a streak of dark spots running down its back seemingly emerge from Lilith, with a second similar creature of pure white following. The spotted leopardess is an emanation from Lilith, signifying the adversities and evil consequences that are her emissaries, working her evil will; the white leopardess is an emanation from Mara, signifying good pursing and overcoming evil. The white constantly opposes the spotted and is predominant. As he nears Bulika, Vane is met by a woman clutching her baby and fleeing from the spotted leopardess. She tells of having fought with the creature and having wounded it, and then explains that it was sent by the princess of Bulika to suck the blood from all newborn children, who then either die or grow up to be idiots. In answer to Vane's query as to why the princess is so cruel, she explains "there is an old prophecy that a child will be the death of her."

Proceeding, Vane enters the mysterious city of Bulika in search of Lilith, whom he now distrusts. The few inhabitants he meets treat him rudely. He sees ahead a white leopardess following a man-like figure that seems to be a two-dimensional shadow; he is Satan, from whose evil machinations positive effects may ensue. More of the Shadow later. Having befriended a woman intimidated by the spotted leopardess, Vane learns from her how the inhabitants live by the crass and inhuman values of materialism.

Determined to help protect the woman's baby from the white leopardess, Vane tries to stand guard at their home, and when a white leopardess emerges carrying a child, he wrestles the child from it. But he is then startled to find the leopardess couching at his feet, wanting to be fondled, and it follows at his heels as he goes on his way. It, however, tries to keep him from the Shadow, and he is pleased to be assured that its intentions were for his good. His adversities have a persistent potential for his spiritual growth, but he has yet to make serious mistakes.

Resuming his purpose to find the princess, Vane enters her castle. The first thing he sees is a spotted leopardess in a cage. Gaining admittance to

18. "Self-denial," *Unspoken Sermons*, 365.

the princess's presence, he is "struck dumb" by her beauty and her seductive advances. Surrounded by materialist values, the temptation to egoism—self-advantage and indulgence—is very strong. "Could such beauty as I saw, and such wickedness as I suspected, exist in the same person?" Vane wonders. She bids him bathe, change into garments she provides, and meet her in a designated chamber. After feasting together upon cakes, fruit, and enchanting wine, she explains how the people of Bulika are evolving to a future perfection, and then details the qualities of the love she demands, offering herself completely to him. The scene epitomizes dominant cultural attitudes that MacDonald saw emerging in his day, and which are many times stronger today.

Lilith fabricates a story explaining how it was Vane found her in a comatose condition before he began to revive her. Undertaking to visit the colony of the hated Little Ones, she is rendered unconscious as a result of trying to cross a stream over which "a certain woman" had cast a spell. Vane has been warned by the raven not to trust anyone who attempts to deceive him; he should be alert to this situation. While the setting of the fantasy is the terrain of the afterlife, the implications for the Christian life here and now are strong.

Something within him does prompt him slightly to distrust her, and he realizes his is an either-or plight: "I felt that, if I did less than loathe her, I should love her." At the moment he was tempted to "love a lie," they are startled by a "frightful roar," and Vane feels it has come from the white leopardess. MacDonald must have in mind such statements of Christ as "if your eye causes you to sin, tear it out. It is better for you to enter the kingdom of God with one eye than with two eyes to be thrown in hell, where the worm does not die and the fire is not quenched. For everyone will be salted with fire."[19]

Lilith's seductive speech in chapter 25 details the various attitudes one can entertain towards oneself. Self-pity, or any suggestion of inferiority, offends the proud nature of the self, which demands complete subservience to its whims. To surrender to the demands of the self issues in a sense of satisfaction and arrogance, to resist them is to encounter inner unrest and rebellion. Perfect love for her, Lilith declares, is complete surrender.

In Lilith's fabricated account of how she came by the emaciated condition in which Vane found her, the "hot stream" that she attempted unsuccessfully to cross suggests the abiding truths of eternal reality. The "certain

19. Mark 9:47–49. Cf., e.g., Matt 5:30; 1 Cor 3:12–15; Heb 12:25–29.

woman" that had cast upon her a stupefying spell is, of course, Mara, who represents the adversities that Providence sets to define the bounds beyond which evil cannot go. Mara's white leopardess, whose roar Vane hears as he is strongly tempted to give himself to Lilith, is another occurrence of providential action, this time being a warning for Vane not to "love a lie." He now realizes, however, that in reviving Lilith as he did he had saved the life of the Little One's "fearful enemy." Egoism for the Christian is a constant temptation; one's conscience warns against it. It is the chief impediment to a Christian's relationship with fellow Christians.

A Battle Royal: Chapters 26–27

In the night Vane is awakened by a stinging pain and sees Lilith standing over him, wiping blood from her mouth: she has again been the vampire sucking his blood. He is now quite aware of her true character and what is happening to him: "I was a tame animal for her to feed upon, a human fountain for a thirst demoniac. She showed me favour the more easily to use me!"

Lilith seems transfigured into the leopardess, and as it flees, Vane dashes after it. Amid a multitude of shadows he sees the spotted leopardess bounding away with a baby in its mouth; the white leopardess accosts it, fights the spotted one, rescues the child, and escapes.

In spite of the fact that Lilith again tries to deceive Vane with a concocted story of how she received her wounds, he does her bidding, thereby completely disobeying the warning that the raven had given him never to obey the behests of a person who has once deceived him. She bids him climb a tree to retrieve a blossom that would heal her scratches. Obeying her, he climbs to near the summit, is seized with a sinking feeling, and finds himself emerging from the water of a stone basin in his own garden, face to face with the raven, who croaks, "I told you so."

The Persian Cat: Chapters 28–29

Coming to himself in the garden of his estate, Vane asks the question, "What does it all mean?' and the raven replies, "Nobody knows what anything is; a man can learn only what a thing means! Whether he does depends on the use he is making of it." The raven is pressing upon Vane the shortcomings of the scientific approach of which he is enamored. It is good at analyzing, but all its analysis is unable to reveal in any metaphysical sense what an object is, and, although science may be adept at revealing an object's function, it is unable to reveal what something *means*. This can only be ascertained by discerning an object's relation to Transcendent Reality, and one discovers that by finding its proper use. No amount of merely analyzing it will do.

In response to Vane's protest that he did intend to do something for the Little Ones, the raven explains that he went about it wrongly. "Had you accepted our invitation, you would have known the right way." But in what sense would Vane have come to know the right way? Does a Christian of dedicated commitment somehow possess superior knowledge? MacDonald indicates here and elsewhere that, when a person is thoroughly intent upon doing God's will and is obeying in love Christ's precepts, that one should trust God to lead rightly. In the poem "Death and Birth" he writes:

> Find the secret—follow and find!
> All forget that lies behind;
> Me, the schools, yourselves forsake;
> In your souls a silence make;
> Hearken till a whisper come,
> Listen, follow, and be dumb.[20]

One can recall the words of Christ: "I am the light of the world; he who follows me will not walk in darkness, but will have the light of life" and David's assertion: "Thou dost show me the path of life." Paul tells the Corinthians that "in every way you were enriched in him with all speech and all knowledge."[21] But Vane's problem continues to be one of self-will: he is still privileging his own judgment rather than simply obeying.

When a Persian cat appears from the shrubbery, the raven takes a book and reads aloud portions from a poem that recounts aspects of how Lilith as Adam's first wife began to lust for power and a luxurious life. The cat's howl and attempted flight reveals her to be an incarnation of Lilith. Addressing her, the raven recounts her history and the nature of her fall, and in doing so reveals himself to be an incarnation, or, perhaps more accurately, an emanation, of Adam.

The raven chooses a mutilated volume from Vane's library and proceeds to read a poem in the presence of Vane and Lilith, the latter now incarnate as a Persian cat. Vane tries to render the poem as best he can, confessing that it is a "poor approximation" of what he actually heard. The

---

20. MacDonald, *Poetical Works*, vol. 2, 24.

21. John 8:12; Ps 16:11; 1 Cor 1:5.

poem recounts Lilith's story and highlights her rebellious attitudes. The final stanza captures what may be said to be the kernel idea of the fantasy:

> Ah, the two worlds! So strangely are they one,
> And yet so measurelessly wide apart!
> Oh, had I lived the bodiless alone
> And from defiling sense held safe my heart,
> Then had I scaped the canker and the smart,
> Scaped life-in-death, scaped misery's endless moan!

The manner in which the Region of the Seven Dimensions—the abode of the eternal verities by which all lives are measured—intermingles with our present world—in which beguiling appearances continually mask enduring realities—is indeed a mystery. When Vane presses the raven for an explanation, he replies, "I am sorry I cannot explain the thing to you, but there is no provision in you for understanding it." He proceeds to remind Vane that "The fact is, no man understands anything; when he knows he does not understand, that is his first tottering step—not toward understanding, but toward the capability of one day understanding."

If Lilith had lived "the bodiless alone," she would have avoided all the misery and suffering she has and must yet endure. One is reminded of Paul's privileging the unseen world over the one seen. He wrote, "Though our outer nature is wasting away, our inner nature is being renewed every day. For this slight momentary affliction is preparing for us an eternal weight of glory beyond all comparison, because we look not the things that are seen but to the things that are unseen; for the things that are seen are transient, but the things that are unseen are eternal."[22]

Vane explains that now at last he understands that the raven "was indeed Adam, the old and the new man, and that his wife, ministering in the house of the dead, was Eve, the mother of us all, the lady of the New Jerusalem." Their repentance has enthroned them as the guardians and caretakers of "house of the dead," to which all must eventually submit to complete the process of becoming new creatures in Christ.

In having Adam affirm that God created man out of "His own endless glory," MacDonald is taking issue with Augustine's affirmation that God created *ex nihilo*, that is, out of nothing. In the novel *Weighed and Wanting* he explains:

---

22. 2 Cor 4:16–18.

I repent me of the ignorance wherein I ever said that God made man out of nothing: there is no nothing out of which to make anything; God is all in all, and he made us out of himself. He who is parted from God has no original nothingness with which to take refuge. He is a live discord, an anti-truth. He is a death fighting against life, and doomed to endless vanity; an opposition to the very power by whose strength yet in him he opposes; a world of contradictions, not greedy after harmony, but greedy for lack of harmony—his being an abyss of positive negation.[23]

Much of MacDonald's theology, including his hope for the eventual salvation of all peoples, rests on this foundation.

Lilith, Adam continues, allied herself with "the great Shadow," that is, Satan, and he "became her slave, and made her queen of hell." The spirit of hell, therefore, is the fallen self, and the nature of hell, for any given individual, is determined by the particular evil that one was committed to. Shades of Dante here.

As Lilith stands displaying her beauty, Adam calls attention to the spot on her side and tells her it will not leave until it has eaten to her heart. The spot, of which there are many references in the text, symbolizes the principle that evil has within itself the seeds of its own destruction. Evil not only has no independent reality, but lives by its parasitical relationship to the good; it also is self-consuming. "Good and not Evil is the Universe," Adam concludes; "the battle between them may last for countless ages, but it must end." However, she utterly spurns his plea for her to repent.

Adam Explains: Chapters 30–31

In the speeches of Adam that follow, much of the theological undergirding of the fantasy becomes clear. The child Lilith is determined to destroy is Lona, the compassionate guardian of the Little Ones who is engaged in rescuing children from Bulika and mothering them. Lilith is persistently trying to destroy her because the ancient prophecy states that her child will effect her demise. Lona symbolizes the good that comes from evil, and the battle between them symbolizes the constant attempt by evil to destroy the virtues that do emerge.

The fantasy, therefore, is an elaborate presentation of the doctrine of the fortunate fall. As we remarked above in our discussion of Vane's visit

23. Chapter 35.

with Mara, it is paradoxically true that evil is necessary for the creation of virtue. An unfallen world with unfallen creatures—Eden—is in a sense sterile; it is unable to produce such virtues as hope—in a perfect world what is there to hope for? The same is true of faith—when God and all good are immediately present, the eye of faith has no function. So with pity—one's neighbors have no lack. And with *agape* love—there is no lack in others for which one need sacrifice to meet. Where evil abounds, grace does much more abound, to paraphrase Paul. Adam remarks that before the fall he and Eve longed to foster Lona, but "we were then unfit to train her."

MacDonald is in a sense repeating what the imagery concerning Mara formerly affirmed. Lona is constantly rescuing babies from Bulika, just as so very often it is adversity that brings people to repentance and faith. But, in spite of Lona's best efforts, some of those rescued—the Little Ones—become lethargic and grow into Bags. MacDonald is keenly aware that in churches there may be some who "go downhill to the animals' country," as he puts it in *The Princess and Curdie.*

Adam rebukes Vane because his philanthropic intentions—his private notions of how to effect good for the Little Ones—are products of his inferior self; his egotism is symbolized by his having found the comatose body of Lilith and revived her. Adam renews his plea for Vane to visit Eve's cottage, but Vane persists in relying upon his own judgment.

Back in the country beyond the mirror, Adam/raven beckons for the horse "that will carry you in the morning." Vane seems to be given a vision of his great capabilities to effect good once he has truly died into life. His infatuation, however, with his own intentions creates within him greed, covetousness, and a desire for possession, and prompts him to defy the raven's commands. As he rides away to follow his own self-generated vision, the steed disintegrates, and he finds himself back in his Evil Wood.

Back with the Lovers and the Bags: Chapters 32–33

As a consequence of his recalcitrant disobedience, Vane incurs severe adversity. After being attacked by a herd of wolves and severely mauled by a multitude of cats, he is captured by a group of giants. The Little Ones, however, rescue him, and he is compassionately ministered to by Lona. Good emerges from adversity, but not without considerable cost.

Lona's concern and merciful care has a spiritually curative effect upon Vane: "Every word she spoke seemed to go straight to my heart, and, like the truth itself, make it purer." He marvels that "such a child should have been born of such a mother." That his spiritual discernment is growing is evident in his correctly understanding the great difference between the purposes of the white and spotted leopardess, together with his growing interest in how the Little Ones are getting the better of the giants, and in his readiness to further the scheme being conceived by the woman from Bulika for the capturing of that stronghold of evil.

To Bulika: Chapters 34–35

Placing great confidence in the ancient prophecy that Lilith is to meet her doom through her daughter, Vane is enthusiastically ready to help further the seemingly fool-hardy task of the Little Ones attacking and conquering Bulika. He reasons: ". . . must not the Little Ones, from a crowd of children, speedily become a youthful people, whose government and influence would be all for righteousness? Ruling the wicked with a rod of iron, would they not be the redemption of the nation?" MacDonald's eschatological vision seems to suggest post-millennialism: the church will itself subdue evil and prepare the world for the coming of Christ and the establishment of the kingdom. "Lona had herself grown a good deal," Vane remarks; the greater the evil, the greater the good that proceeds from it. One cannot but wonder, were he living in the twenty-first century rather than in the nineteenth—writing as he was some twenty years before the outbreak of World War I and all the horrendous outbreaks of evil that followed in the twentieth century—if he would still hold that view.

The truths upon which he has a firm hold, however—that true good does continually proceed from the machinations of evil, and that evil for all its horrendousness nevertheless has no independent reality—are as inviolable now as they were in the Victorian period.

Admirable as Vane's purposes may be, his spiritual deficiencies remain. He confesses to his personal ambition to rule with Lona should Bulika be conquered, and to a dream of "opening a commerce in gems between the two worlds." He is also quite willing to postpone any attempt to secure water for the Little Ones. Nevertheless, he and Lona form a bond that successfully leads a charge of the Little Ones, and Bulika is captured.

Mother and Daughter: Chapter 36

As the self-absorbed Lilith strives to contemplate her own beauty, she quakes as she catches sight of the approaching army of Little Ones. Simultaneously, the dark spot on her side rapidly grows and the spotted leopardess dies. No sooner does Lona burst upon the scene longing to embrace her mother when Lilith seizes her in hatred and dashes her on the marble floor, effecting her demise.

The prophecy was that Lilith would be killed by her child; the opposite seems to have happened. How so? Since the reign of Lilith has been overcome, and, as she is to be taken to Eve's house, she is on the way to being saved; Lona has been the moving force in her conquest. The spot on Lilith's side signifies her evil character; its growth signifies the inevitability of its demise: evil has no independent reality, but is parasitical. It is inevitable that at the moment evil is vanquished the good that comes from evil disappears; it no longer has its source. Hence Lona's death. Thus the prophecy is being fulfilled.

All the while the sun is shining brightly upon the scene. The frequent appearances of the moon in the fantasy, and now at this crucial moment the fervent beams of the sun, suggest the overarching presence of God working out the divine purposes while at the same time contemplating and honoring human instrumentality.

At the Houses of Bitterness and Death: Chapters 37–40

Odu, one of the Little Ones, recounts how the Shadow came upon him after the capture of Lilith and attempted to possess his inner being. He was repulsed by the "bad" feeling that came over him, and ran away. The Shadow is Satan, a shadow because, as we have remarked before, evil has no independent reality. It has no "thick," Odu explains. That the image has only two dimensions underscores its contrast to the "seven dimensions" of spiritual reality.

The party proceeds to take Lilith to the House of Bitterness. The next step in her spiritual journey from the depths of her evil reign is the essential one of thorough repentance. The House of Bitterness necessarily stands between the Evil Wood and Eve's House.

That repentance is essential, very possibly painful, but has a compassionate intention and a glorious outcome, is all imaged forth both in the dread the Little Ones express at the prospect of encountering Mara and in Mara's direct statements. Since Lilith will not "yield to gentler measures," Mara explains, "harder must have their turn. I must do what I can to made her repent. . . . It would be cruel to hurt her too little." The divine presence is overseeing Lilith, Mara affirms, but she is not "with Him."

In these chapters the procession composed of the Little Ones and led by Vane brings the emaciated Lilith to Mara's House of Bitterness. After Mara's loving and persistent working with her, Lilith capitulates, agrees to die into life, and is taken to Eve's cemetery to sleep the sanctifying sleep. Lilith's true self—that self which God intended at her creation—triumphs over the self she had made herself to become. This repentance and surrender necessarily precede the final transformation of the person that will take place in Eve's house.

The scene in which Mara works patiently with Lilith to effect her surrender is shaped by many of MacDonald's central theological convictions. The theme of the multiple selves was introduced early in the text in chapter 6. There Mr. Raven explains:

> Upon occasion . . . it is more convenient to put one's bird-self in front. Every one, as you ought to know, has a beast-self—and a bird-self, and a stupid fish-self, ay, and a creeping serpent self too—which it takes a deal of crushing to kill! In truth he has also a tree-self and a crystal-self, and I don't know how many selves more—all to get into harmony. You can tell what sort a man is by his creature that comes oftenest to the front.

In these chapters, the theme of multiple selves centers upon the contrast between the ideal self, which is God's original idea of the individual, versus the corrupted self that the individual has effected through pitting her own will against that of God's. Lilith here symbolizes the composite of recalcitrant fallen souls. Mara gently urges her, "Will you turn away from the wicked things you have been doing so long?" to which Lilith replies, "I will not. I will be myself and not another." Mara responds, "Alas, you are another now, not yourself! Will you not be your real self?" When Lilith insists ". . . you shall not compel me to anything against my will," Mara explains: "Such a compulsion would be without value. But there is a light that goes deeper than the will, a light that lights up the darkness behind it: that light can change your will, can make it truly yours and not another's—not the

Shadow's. Into the created can pour itself the creating will, and so redeem it." In MacDonald's thought, the individual will is most certainly free, but it may not ultimately be so. God finally may exercise the power to override the human will in order to free it from enslavement to Satan.

For what is at the heart of the matter is the struggle between God and Satan. The rebellious human will is in bondage to Satan ("The Shadow" in MacDonald's imagery), and that enslavement can be broken. One recalls Christ's statement, "Every one who commits sin is slave to sin. The slave does not continue in the house forever; the son continues for ever. So if the son makes you free, you will be free indeed."[24]

As Lilith lies prone on a settle (a long bench) surrounded by "cloudy presences," a slowworm appears and proceeds to creep into the fire on the hearth. Shortly thereafter it emerges "white-hot, vivid as incandescent silver, the live heart of essential fire," and creeps along the folds of Lilith's robe to pass into the black spot on her side, "piercing through the joints and marrow to the thoughts and intents of the heart." Lilith has a seizure. "She is seeing herself!" Mara exclaims. "She is far away from us, afar in the hell of her self-consciousness. The central fire of the universe is radiating into her the knowledge of good and evil, the knowledge of what she is. . . . Her torment is that she is what she is."

The worm and fire imagery recalls Christ's statement that hell is the place where "the worm does not die, and the fire is not quenched."[25] Mac-Donald apparently equates the worm with the soul and the fire with the essential glory of God. In the presence of God's holiness the soul receives clear-sighted knowledge both of the moral beauty of the ideal self God intended and the moral horror of the corrupt entity it has made itself to be.

Lilith continues to resist Mara's efforts. She tries to blame God for having made her as she is: "He alone is to blame for what I am!" she cries. But her seeing herself as victim is totally unacceptable. She is herself completely responsible for what she has become. God, however, is willing and able to remake her, restoring her to her true original self.

Finally, Lilith ostensibly gives up. But Mara, suspecting that her submission is not yet thorough, says, "Begin, then, and set right in the place of wrong." For this Lilith must open her hand, and, in spite of Mara's insisting that she can, she pleads she cannot do it. The result is that Lilith undergoes a still more fearful experience: she is immersed in the "outer darkness."

24. John 8:34–36.
25. Mark 9:48.

At last she asks for death. Mara then assures her, "Thou shalt die out of death into life. Now is the Life for, that never was against thee!" The great gospel truth finally registers, that God is never against the sinner, nor is he interested in punishment for punishment's sake. The soul's true enemy is its own self-will. Lilith weeps.

Simultaneously, while Vane is watching all that is taking place, he realizes something is taking place within himself: "Something began to depart from me. A sense of cold, yet not what we call cold, crept, not into, but out of my being." Symbolically, Vane by his actions has participated in the spirit of self-centeredness that Lilith represents, and her capitulation is tantamount to his own.

The party now leaves the House of Bitterness to proceed to Eve's Cemetery. Springlike gladness accompanies them, together with showers that issue in flowing rivers. Waters under the earth are awakened. One recalls the water imagery that often in Scripture accompanies eschatological scenes, such as the mighty river that flows from the temple in the closing of the book of Ezekiel, or the river that flows from the throne of God in the book of Revelation.[26] Water suggests the waters of abundant life.

They are greeted happily by Adam and Eve. Still unable to open her hand, Lilith pleads with Adam to help her. He brings his sword and severs it. Perhaps MacDonald wants his readers to see the truth that God will do for persons what they absolutely cannot do for themselves. To recall a line from *King Lear*, the gods "made them honors of men's impossibilities."[27] God does not violate the human will, but the will has its limitations. What Mara told Lilith earlier applies: "There is a light that goes deeper than the will, a light that lights up the darkness behind it: that light can change your will, can make it truly yours and not another's—not the Shadow's." The statement has large theological ramifications.

We now learn Mara is Eve's daughter. Symbolically, Eve through her Edenic disobedience brought bitterness and grief into the world. But Mara is the grief that accompanies repentance. She stands for all adverse circumstances and heartaches that issue in repentance. Formerly we learned that Lona is Lilith's daughter: the rebellious human will occasions the work of redemptive grace. Eve tells Lilith: "Death shall be the atonemaker; you shall sleep together." The righting of all wrongs and complete reconciliation is ahead for them in Eve's chambers. Evil thus completely replaced with good,

26. Cf. Ezek 47:1–12; Rev 22:1–2.
27. IV.6.

the Shadow itself shall sleep. A former statement of Adam's clarifies: "An-nihilation itself is no death to evil. Only good where evil was, is evil dead. An evil thing must live with its evil until it chooses to be good. That alone is the slaying of evil."[28] Eve and Mara, Lilith and Lona, together with the Shadow, suggest the history and destiny of created beings.

Vane is not only an engrossed observer of the phases of Lilith's ago-nies. What he is seeing mirrors his own experience. The Evil Wood, one remembers, is shaped by his own consciousness, and Lilith, as we noted in the early scene in which he revives her, is in part his own depraved self. Certain moments in the text remind the reader of this identification. When Lilith is reliving "a tale about herself," Vane remarks: ". . . the language seemed the primeval shape of one I know well, and the forms to belong to dreams which had once been mine. . . . vices too, I could not help suspect-ing—with which I was unacquainted." It is as though Vane is entering his subconscious and learning aspects of himself of which he was unaware.

Vane also identifies with Lilith when her further persistence precipi-tates an inner dialogue that issues in her being confronted by the threat of annihilation. He states: "Gradually my soul grew aware of an invisible darkness. . . . a horrible Nothingness. . . . the border of its being that was yet no being, touched me, and for one ghastly instant I seemed alone with Death Absolute."

When at last she has a vision of "splendent beauty"—the self God had intended her to be, compared with what she is—Lilith completely capitu-lates: "you have conquered," she says in "prideful humility." When Mara tells her she must then begin to "set right in the place of wrong," she finds she cannot open her hand.

The closed hand is evidently an important image, for the narrative makes much of it. It signifies Lilith's inability finally to undo all the evil she is responsible for. What is required before the process of receiving the new self begins is a complete disowning of one's past, a letting go of all one has done, and what one has done is the real definition of what a person is. The last vestiges of pride must be utterly forsaken.

For her inability to persist in trying to open her hand herself, she experiences the uttermost state of *"Life in Death,"* but even this is of no avail, and her own efforts fail her: "She had tried her hardest to unmake herself, and could not! She was a dead life! she must *be*" [italics his]. In her extremity, she yields and is transformed. In a stirring passage, we read

28. Chapter 30.

how "Morn, with the Spring in her arms" flows through the opened door to enfold her: she is brought into harmony with eternal Being. The chapter ends with Mara embracing and kissing Lilith, promising that she will "die out of death into life," and there follows a soft breeze and a healing rain.

The entire party now proceeds to Eve's house, Mara safely leading the way through a terrain beset with phantom monsters. Mara meets her mother, Eve (it is Eve who originally brought suffering into the world), who gladly welcomes all to the House of Death. Adam and Eve take Lilith, whose spirit is still resisting them, to the couch in the chamber of death upon which she must sleep. One by one the Little Ones obediently choose couches and quickly fall asleep. Those whose new birth has begun on earth gladly accept the glorifying sleep.

Finally, Lilith asks Adam to sever her hand, which, as soon as he does, she succumbs to sleep. Once the willingness is secured, the grace of God completes the process of a thorough obliteration of what one formerly was and did.

The chapter contains several allusions to "the great Shadow." When Lilith asks to be killed, Eve tells her she cannot. "You shall not go to the Shadow. . . . Even now is his head under my heel."[29] Later Adam tells her: "When the Shadow comes here, it will be to lie down and sleep also—His hour will come, and he knows it well." Apparently even Satan—Lucifer—will be restored to that which he was before he fell.

I Am Sent: Chapter 41

All have been invited to sleep, except Vane. His flaw has been lack of obedience—pitting his own judgment over against divine authority—and he must first demonstrate his complete capitulation to higher wisdom.

Vane's identification with Lilith as a symbol of his depraved self is underscored by the task Adam gives Vane to perform. He must show his obedience by taking Lilith's severed hand and burying it at a select spot in the desert. Adam's instructions are very explicit and precise. Vane will find the proper place by following the sound of flowing waters. In other words, he must give complete deference to spiritual truths. Burying the hand suggests his own entire disowning of his past.

On his way he successfully resists various forms of his former weaknesses. A phantom of Lilith appears, enticing, then threatening him; he

29. Gen 3:15.

shuns her. One that appears to be Mara bids him rest while she takes charge of his burden; weary though he is, Vane does not turn aside. The Shadow itself confronts him and for a fearful moment passes through him, to no avail. Finally attaining to the designated place, he fulfills the task assigned him. His full obedience has been demonstrated.

Vane Sleeps the Sleep: Chapter 42

On the way back to Eve's cottage, Vane meets a grieving, aged man who complains he has asked Eve to die and has been refused. He wants to die because he has lost any love for life itself. He is, in short, suicidal. Vane tells him that the privilege to die is granted only to those who have a passion for life.

Vane's advice to him is: "Go to the Lady of Sorrow, and 'take with both hands' what she will give you." Instead of wanting to die and escape adversity, wisdom is to try heartily to affirm the hardships of life in order to receive the good that is inherent in them.[30] Vane feels his advice is unheeded, but he goes on his way confident that "Mara would find him." Hardships must be allowed to accomplish the spiritual purposes they were sent to effect.

Entering the house of death, Vane is haunted by a sense of loneliness until he meets Lona, who urges him to come with her, affirming she "cannot rest until you are with me," and they retire in adjacent beds. It is the good that comes from evil—Lona—that has finally brought him to the death that will effect the full emergence of his true self. That Vane now deeply loves Lona rather then—as formerly—Lilith, reveals his commitment to compassion and loving action, those efforts that assist the process of bringing good out of evil.

Adam comes, and he hears Eve singing "sweet and soft and low" one of MacDonald's better quatrains:

> Many a wrong, and its curing song,
> Many a road, and many an inn,
> Room to roam, but only one home
> For all the world to win.

---

30. James writes: "Count it all joy, my brothers, when you meet trials of various kinds, for you know that the testing of your faith produces steadfastness . . ." (1:2–3), and Paul writes: "For while we are still in this tent, we groan, being burdened—not that we would be unclothed, but that we would be further clothed, so that what is mortal may be swallowed up by life" (2 Cor 5:4).

And Adam reaffirms the principle: "Every creature must one night yield himself and lie down . . . he was made for liberty, and must not be left a slave."

On Vane's other side lies Lilith, whom Adam identifies as Vane's mother, and thus the text reiterates the symbolism we have noted above: Lilith signifies, among other aspects of evil, Vane's depraved self. Adam continues, anticipating Lilith's awakening: "Then she will open her eyes, behold on one side her husband, on the other her son—and rise and exceed them to go to a father and a brother more to her than they." Lilith's husband is Adam, her son Vane, and the greater father and brother are God the Father and Christ the Son.

The Dreams That Came: Chapter 43

The next phase in Vane's birthing process is for him to confront all the wrongs he had ever done, "confessing, abjuring, lamenting the dead, making atonement with each person I had injured, hurt, or offended." He does it in the ecstasy of the spirit of love: "Love was my life! Love was to me, as to him that made me, all in all." He is growing less and less conscious of himself, more and more conscious of pure bliss.

Curiously, his euphoria is followed by a bout of depression and fright;[31] he is desolate and alone, all the beds are empty. Dashing out, running across the moor and fording streams, he searches desperately for his companions, when he is met by Adam. In desperation questioning him as to where the dead have gone, Vane is told he has been dreaming: the others are still in their couches beside him.

The passage that follows introduces one of the issues with which MacDonald was beset over his lifetime: how can one know whether one's dreams have any truth in them? The pure and upright imagination can conjure magnificent vistas and blissful situations: is it all chimeras, foolish and impossible fantasies? Can the imagination of man exceed and outdo the capabilities of God? Or will they some day be realized?[32] Will the hopes expressed in this entire work be realized, or are they simply vain (Vane) desires?

---

31. MacDonald himself was beset with alternating bouts of euphoria and depression, and they intensified in his later years.

32. Cf. MacDonald, *Diary of an Old Soul*, April 2, 3, 5.

To Vane's urgent questioning Adam responds that, until one's prior nature is quite dead, one cannot discern the true from the false. Until then, a certain quantity of doubt and error is inevitable and not blameworthy. Adam explains:

> Thou hast not yet looked the Truth in the face, hast as yet at best but seen him through a cloud. That which thou seest not, and never didst see save in a glass darkly—that which, indeed, never can be known save by its innate splendour shining straight into pure eyes—that thou canst not but doubt, and art blameless in doubting until thou seest it face to face, when thou wilt no longer be able to doubt it. But to him who has once seen even a shadow only of the truth, and . . . tries to obey it—to him . . . the Truth himself, will come, . . . and abide with him for ever.

One must be content to live in the realm of uncertainty and earnestly try to obey the truth one sees. To such more truth will come; on that day when one sees God face to face, the truth will be forever clear, and doubt will be forever dead.

Then Adam disappears. Vane begins to wander and, on a whim, jumps into a pit. He now finds himself back in the garret of his house. Desperately trying to return to be beside Lona, he is unable to do so and falls into another depressive state.

The Journey to the City: Chapters 44–46

After four nights Vane awakes indeed and with joy finds himself again by Lona's side. Adam, Eve, and Mara appear and assure them they have now indeed "died into life, and will die no more, you have only to keep dead." In the distance the golden cock grows, heralding the approaching dawn of "the day eternal," while one by one the Little Ones joyously awake.

Adam tells Vane, "Now you have only to live, and that you must, with all your blessed might. The more you live, the stronger you become to live." The passage at the beginning of chapter 45, one of the finest I think that MacDonald wrote, describes a part of what he feels a greater fullness of life means: "A wondrous change had passed upon the world—or was it not rather that a change more marvelous had taken place in us? . . . Every growing thing showed me by its shape and colour, its indwelling idea—the informing thought, that is, which was its being, and sent it out." The meanings with which God has invested things—meanings the mind formerly had longed to grasp but could only guess—now are crystal clear.

Not only so, but Vane now feels a completely harmonious relation with all living things; the schism that humans feel between them and the created world no longer exists. "I lived in everything, everything entered and lived in me. To be aware of a thing, was to know its life at once and mine, to know whence we came, and where we were at home—was to know that we are all what we are, because Another is what he is!" The sacramental energies resident in the world have perfect interaction with Vane's innermost being.

MacDonald felt that everything in one's life, objects and incidents alike, have the potential to function as sacraments, that is, they have the potential to convey grace. A great deal of one's spiritual health in this life consists in feeling this harmony as much as one can.

As the party proceeds, they are gripped with a feeling of constant increase and joyous expectation:

> . . . something more than the sun, greater than the light, is coming, is coming—none the less surely coming that it is long upon the road! What matters to-day or to-morrow, or then thousand years to Life himself, to Love himself! He is coming, is coming, and the necks of all humanity are stretched out to see him come! Every morning will they thus outstretch themselves, every evening will they droop and wait—until he comes.

Their expectation is riveted upon the appearance of God in Christ, "the master-minister of the human tabernacle," at his Second Coming.[33] As they come to within sight of the city, the New Jerusalem, Vane overhears the Little Ones, thrilling with delight, discussing their encounter with "the beautifullest man" who assures them in their baby talk, "Ou's all mine's, 'ickle ones: come along!" The figure is Christ. MacDonald is avoiding any attempt to become didactic in making theological statements about Christ by thus presenting him through the eyes of the "most childish" of the party, but his statement is, nevertheless, a sweepingly comprehensive one. All things are from Christ and are in his keeping. He is "the master-mind" of the universe, and all that has been envisioned in this work has ultimately been engineered by him.

MacDonald's depictions of God are never of a grand figure on a grand throne, but rather of a glorious being for whom one increasingly longs with a longing that increases as knowledge grows. "But the path of the just is

33. The text echoes Rom 8:19–23; 1 Cor 15:20–28.

as the shining light, that shineth more and more unto the perfect day"[34] is no doubt one of the verses that fed his imagination as he shaped *Lilith*. MacDonald is playing a game of brinksmanship with the beatific vision, stopping short of attempting something akin to Dante's vision at the conclusion of *The Paradisio*. He is keenly aware that any imaginative attempts to see beyond a point are futile.

This spirit of something beyond description that is ever increasing in delight and never reaching stasis is a frequent aspect of MacDonald's writings whenever he contemplates the Christian's future. The ending of "The Golden Key" is another example. In *Diary of an Old Soul* he wrote:

> Love will not backward sigh, but forward strain,
> On in the tale still telling, never told.[35]

As the party rushes onward, their delight in the beauties they now perceive surrounding them reach a peak as they see atop a solitary mountain a great city, with "palace and precipice mingled in a seeming chaos of broken shadow and shine." It is the Zion of Christian promise and longing. Their approach to the city is replete with intense delights. But as they climb towards the throne of the Ancient of Days, Vane feels "a hand, warm and strong" drawing him through a door, and he suddenly finds himself back in his library on his estate.

The "Endless Ending": Chapter 47

Some critics find the final chapter unsettling, posing problems that question MacDonald's faith in the exalted vision that he has concluded. Robert Woolf concludes that he finally was disillusioned with his entire system of thought.[36] Why does Vane now have "moments of doubt"? And why does he vow never again to seek the mirror or "go out again by that door"?

It should be noted that the doubts in question here are not as to the existence of God, but rather as to the validity of his vision. Is its optimism as to the universal triumph of good valid? To the reflection of some of his doubting friends, such as Ruskin, that his vision was too good to be true, MacDonald was fond of saying, "It is so good, it has to be true."

---

34. Prov 4:18 KJV.

35. April 4.

36. Wolff, *The Golden Key*, 369–370.

MacDonald in utter honesty is here posing again the question he asked in chapter 43: can the imagination of good and earnest people outdo the creating power of God? His final answer is simply to affirm that, as God is the source of the human mind, so is he the source of the dream: "Whence came the fantasia? . . . Didst *thou* say, in the dark of thy own unconscious self, 'Let beauty be, let truth seem!' and straightway beauty was, and truth but seemed?" The implied answer is that God instilled within the mind longings for both beauty and truth. Beauty surrounds us; why does truth only seem? One should recall Adam's response to Vane's questionings in the prior chapter. Truth can only seem to beings not yet themselves completely true. "The hour will come, and that ere long, when, being true, thou shalt behold the very truth, and doubt will be for ever dead . . ." Ultimate Truth is of such ineffable splendor our fallen minds cannot begin to comprehend it. All visions, including the one detailed in this work, are therefore tentative.

Vane, his life on earth still ahead of him, is in his fallen state not yet completely true. Trials yet await him. But he has achieved that measure of spiritual maturity that waits entirely upon the will of God and thus resists impulses merely to satisfy a sensual curiosity. He will not go out of "that door" again because to do so would be tantamount to questioning the reality of what he has experienced, or to probe it simply for sake of indulging himself or gaining information. "All the days of my appointed time will I wait till my change come" echoes the attitude of Job.[37] Vane is satisfied simply to be patient and obedient, trusting whatever the Giver bestows.

We have said in the Introduction that MacDonald placed in the earlier manuscripts of *Lilith* a great many references to Dante's *The Divine Comedy* which he expunged from the final manuscript, retaining only three. The third occurs near the beginning of chapter 45 in the passage in which Vane exalts in the newfound harmony he feels with the world around him. It reads:

> When a little breeze brushing a bush of heather set its purple bells a ringing, I was myself in the joy of the bells, myself in the joy of the breeze to which responded their sweet *tintinning*, myself in the joy of the sense, and of the soul that received all the joys together.

In a footnote the coined word is attributed to Del Paradiso X.142. Why does MacDonald include at this point in his narrative this seemingly obscure reference? It seems unnecessary. A look into Dante's text, however,

---

37. Job 14:14 KJV.

suggests a reason. Dante's coined word occurs at that point when Dante is in the presence of Thomas Aquinas, who introduces him to a circle of leading theologians. Last, and closest to him, is Sigier of Brabant. This is remarkable, simply because during their lifetimes on earth Sigier vehemently opposed Aquinas in several famous public debates. Aquinas saw him as epitomizing falsehood, not truth. But now, St. Thomas praises him:

> It's the eternal light of Sigier, who,
> Lecturing down in Straw Street, hammered home
> Invidious truths, as logic taught him to.[38]

In other words, these two fierce questors for truth were, while on earth, avowed opponents, but now they are harmoniously allied. Perhaps MacDonald is slyly suggesting that he and Dante, so widely differing on their views of the nature of eternal damnation, will in the hereafter be closely allied as blessed friends.

38. Sayers, ed., *Paradise*, x.136–38.

Bibliography

Bettelheim, Bruno. *The Uses of Enchantment*. New York: Vintage, 2010.

Dostoevsky, Fyodor. *The Brothers Karamazov*. New York: Barnes & Noble, 2004.

Gill, Stephen, ed. *William Wordsworth*. Oxford: Oxford University Press, 1984.

Grant, John E., ed. *Blake's Poetry and Designs*. New York: Norton, 1979.

Hart, David Bentley. *The Doors of the Sea: Where Was God in the Tsunami?* Grand Rapids: Eerdmans, 2005.

Hein, Rolland, ed. *The Heart of George MacDonald*. Vancouver, BC: Regent, 1997.

———. *Lilith: A Variorum Edition*. 2 vols. Whitethorn, CA: Johannesen, 1997.

Hooper, Walter, ed. *They Stand Together: The Letters of C. S. Lewis to Arthur Greeves*. London: Collins, 1979.

Johnson, Mary Lynn, and John E. Grant, ed. *Blake's Poetry and Designs*. New York: Norton, 2007.

Johnson, Thomas H., ed. *The Complete Poems of Emily Dickinson*. New York: Little, Brown, 1960.

Knight, Ralph, ed. *Songs and Poems of Robert Burns*. Lanham, MD: Rowman and Littlefield, 1956.

Lewis, C. S. *An Experiment in Criticism*. Cambridge: Cambridge University Press, 1965.

———. *George MacDonald: An Anthology*. New York: Macmillan, 1948.

———. *The Great Divorce*. New York: HarperOne, 1946.

———. *Miracles*. New York: Macmillan, 1953.

Sayers, Dorothy, ed. *The Comedy of Dante Alighieri: Hell*. New York: Penguin, 1949.

———. *The Comedy of Dante Alighieri: Paradise*. New York: Penguin, 1962.

MacDonald, George. *At the Back of the North Wind*. Vestal, NY: Anamchara, 2011.

———. *Diary of an Old Soul*. Minneapolis: Augsburg, 1975.

———. *The Complete Fairy Tales*. New York: Penguin, 1999.

———. *Lilith*. Grand Rapids: Eerdmans, 2000.

———. *Paul Faber, Surgeon*. Whitethorn, CA: Johannesen, 1992.

———. *Phantastes*. Edited by Nick Page. London: Paternoster, 2008.

———. Preface, *Letters from Hell*. MacMillan, 1911.

———. *Poetical Works*. 2 vols. London: Chatto & Windus, 1893.

———. *The Princess and Curdie*. New York: Dell, 1986.

———. *The Princess and the Goblin*. New York: Dell, 1986.

———. *Unspoken Sermons*. Whitethorn, CA: Johannesen, 1997.

———. *The Wise Woman*. Grand Rapids: Eerdmans, 1980.

MacDonald, Greville. *George MacDonald and His Wife*. London: Allen & Unwin, 1924.

Bibliography

Masefield, John. *Poems*. New York: Macmillian, 1935.

Muir, Edwin. *Collected Poems*. New York: Grove, 1957.

Rilke, Rainer Maria. *Letters to a Young Poet*. New York: Norton, 1934.

Tolkien, J. R .R. *The Tolkien Reader*. New York: Ballantine, 1966.

Wolff, Robert Lee. *The Golden Key*. New Haven, CT: Yale University Press, 1961.

www.ingramcontent.com/pod-product-compliance
Lightning Source LLC
Chambersburg PA
CBHW032006010726
47493CB00007B/2286